A Shimmer on the horizon

# A Shimmer on the horizon

## Philip Teece

ORCA BOOK PUBLISHERS

Copyright © 1999  Philip Teece

**Canadian Cataloguing in Publication Data**
Teece, Philip,
A shimmer on the horizon

ISBN 1-55143-140-8

1. Sailing – British Columbia – Pacific Coast.  2. Pacific Coast (B.C.) – Description and travel.  I. Title.
GV815.T432 1999   797.1'24'097111   C99–910130-7

**Library of Congress Catalog Card Number:** 98-83020


Canadä
Orca Book Publishers gratefully acknowledges the support of our publishing programs provided by the following agencies: the Department of Canadian Heritage, The Canada Council for the Arts, and the British Columbia Arts Council.

Cover design by Christine Toller
Cover photograph and interior illustrations by the author
Endpaper chart reproduced with the permission of the Canadian Hydrographic Service ©1999 Her Majesty in Right of Canada, Department of Fisheries and Oceans.
Printed and bound in Canada


**Orca Book Publishers**        **Orca Book Publishers**
PO Box 5626, Station B          PO Box 468
Victoria, BC  Canada            Custer, WA   USA
V8R 6S4                         98240-0468

01 00 99   5  4  3  2  1

This book is for Mary,
who, after her first reading of the manuscript, said
"Hey, this is kind of a love story!"

# Contents

# Prelude

 I am flat on my back in tall brown grass. The air is motionless and hot, and the slope beneath me has a southward tilt, inclining me toward the sun. I lie very still. On some bush or blossom very close to my ear a bee is humming a sleepy tune.

This sun-drenched point of land is situated on the upper reaches of the North American west coast. I am on one of a mass of islands 150 miles north of my home port, Victoria, British Columbia. Desolation Sound, the usual limit of most yachtsmen's explorations up this coast, lies a long day's sail south of my resting place in this grassy bower.

People farther south hold a stereotyped image of this part of the BC coast: this far north of Victoria and Vancouver, beyond the normal range of most summer cruising sailors, the clouds hang low and the climate is cool and wet.

Here I recline, however, daydreaming amid the fragrance of sundried wildflowers on the southernmost point of Sonora Island. For most of the week I've been loafing about on this bright, quiet slope, transfixed by the improbable dreamscape that I survey from my perch on the headland.

Immediately below me, viewed between my feet as I lie in the grass, a foamy jet of current tumbles between the narrow gateway of rocks at Hole-in-the-Wall. In the hot, transparent air I feel that I could almost reach across that passageway to touch the high facing mountainside on Maurelle Island.

Only a stone's throw further, where the channel turns and meanders southward, the clustered green knobs of the Octopus Islands are a handful of emeralds spilled onto the water's blue surface. Their firred crests rise brightly into the warm light, separated by slender, curving corridors of sea. More distant still, these same waters stretch lazily between the lush walls of Quadra and Maurelle islands until they pour into the intriguing gap of Surge Narrows.

Winding blue waterways among islands that throng beneath the sun — for me these have always been the elements of a dream that is both powerful and elusive.

In a previous book, *A Dream of Islands*, I described my long search, aboard my little sloop *Galadriel*, for that elusive "something" that always seemed to lie among islands half-hidden in the mist at sunset.

A lot more searching, not without moments of discomfort and fear, has been my happy lot in the years since the little adventures of that book. The diminutive *Galadriel*, now three decades old and much smaller and more primitive than most cruising sailboats of the nineties, continues to be my magic carpet for the search.

Occasionally the elusive object of my quest has seemed very close at hand. At a few rare, special moments — usually in the silence among islands, but once in an offshore gale — I've been granted a fleeting contact with the "something" that I've sought.

Or maybe it was not actually the thing that I had been seeking but, instead, the tantalizing whisper of "something" even better.

# Hiatus

Once, for a year or two, I almost lost the desire to go sailing.

It was a time when nothing seemed to interest me very much. Perhaps I am not the first person who has ever discovered the dark place into which one can stray after the dissolution of a long marriage.

I had been married for nearly three decades and during many happy years the relationship had been very rich and fine. Although my frequent ventures among the British Columbia islands in a small boat were a solo passion, the return to my companion waiting at home was always the central joy of every voyage.

Yet life is an evolution in which nothing remains forever unchanged. Even two people who have travelled so very closely together may surprise each other by their choices when a fork in the road is met. In our two lives, beyond our expectation, there came eventually an unforeseen division of our ways.

For a long while the sorrow of this parting and the irreversible finality of divorce sent out a wave of shock that permeated everything. Books that I read gave me no enjoyment, the subtle splendor of an ocean sunset left me unmoved, the blaze of stars overhead on a fine dark summer night scarcely induced me to look up. Even the beckoning ghosts of islands lying dim on the evening horizon no longer held a siren attraction. Life seemed to have stopped.

A kind of spiritual paralysis held me in its cold grip. I ceased doing things; I no longer felt joy. A frightening lack of perspective closed about me, surrounding me with a grey horizon beyond which I could see nothing.

On a late autumn afternoon, finally, the natural environment itself played a hand and sent a ripple of movement into the dead stillness of my life. After weeks of icy rain and wintry gales, November suddenly relented. One day dawned warm and summery. The crisp, bright glory of it was like an electric shock that galvanized me into action. I launched the dinghy, excavated the oars from a locker deep in *Galadriel*'s bilge, and in bright sunshine rowed out into the waters of my home port in Oak Bay on the southeast tip of Vancouver Island.

To be afloat again, even in a mere nutshell of a dinghy, was strangely comforting.

I sometimes wonder if any form of boating is so perfectly satisfying as the childlike fun of simply messing about in a rowboat. For the first time in months I actually felt something: the pleasurable stretching of my back and shoulder muscles as I pulled the oars. The chuckle of water around the dinghy's lapstrake waterline was a delight, too.

As I rowed away from the dock, I looked at *Galadriel*, lying alongside with the canvas cover lashed down over her cockpit. She seemed small (she is only an eighteen-foot sailboat) and a bit shabby after my recent months of neglect. But I found myself thinking of the twenty-five good years of inter-island pottering that had passed beneath her shallow bilge keels.

Out on the bay I lay into my rowing with increasing vigor. The seven-foot dinghy fairly skipped along, leaving a broad, straight trail of bubbles astern. Passing beyond the outermost of the moored yachts I exerted myself even more strenuously, feeling the catharsis of athletic effort. A dinghy is no racing craft, but suddenly I was well into Olympic training.

In the shallows along Mary Tod Island I slowed to a drift. The sprint had done me good, but now my mood changed. Suspended mere inches above a sandy, sunlit bottom, I let the hint of a breeze carry me slowly, droplets from the blades of my stowed oars leaving a dotted line of tiny beads on the glassy surface.

Nearby a dainty black coot eyed me carefully, a bit suspicious of the fact that his idle paddling was not quite sufficient to prevent my dinghy's windborne drift from slowly closing the gap between us. Slowly, very slowly, our

separation narrowed, to ten feet, to six feet, to an arm's length, and still the little black dumpling did not move. He peered up trustingly at me with a wide red eye. For the first time in months I was not consciously aware of my own mood. It must have been gentle, for the coot felt no urgent concern about my nearness.

I soon drifted past, and eventually the forefoot of the dinghy crunched ashore on one of the island's swatches of gravel beach.

Mary Tod is a small miracle of a place. Only a few hundred yards from the shore and within sight of a busy marina, it is a classic desert isle, an empty little world where the silence allows one to hear the rattle of the windblown grass. I found myself eagerly clambering up the face of its rocky western bluff and then striding across one of its scrub-fringed meadows. Sparrows chirped at me from the tangled oak underbrush as I passed.

Hiking over the island's low crown I walked down onto the eastward-facing flats, out of sight of the marina and town. On this side one might be a thousand miles from civilization, especially on a late autumn or early winter day such as this. I was reminded of the season when a low band of cloud drew a fast-moving curtain of cool shadow first over the island's central ridge, and then down across the grassy field in which I stood. A hundred yards eastward the sea still sparkled in brilliant sunlight.

Then in the west the clouds quickly shifted again, throwing a dazzling spotlight upon me. In another moment the whole island basked in warmth and light; summer-in-

November had returned.

On the island's eastern edge a sheltered crescent of sand attracted me. I walked along the curve of its high-tide dune and sat down on a large driftwood log. It was quiet and warm here at the bottom of the leeward slope, and before me lay a sea that was calm all the way across to the clustered Discovery and Chatham islands. Feeling the unseasonable hint of actual sunburn on my face, I watched a fascinating kaleidoscope of changing shade and light on those shores two miles away.

Then suddenly, at least for the fleeting moment, it was given to me — the gift of joy that I had almost forgotten.

I felt the paradoxical combination of quietude and excitement that islands and the sea had always inspired. Even though I was alone, bereft, adrift, this magic still lay in wait for me in a silent place where the surf washed up onto a pebbled shore. For a moment I might almost have shouted my pleasure. Perhaps I did; there was no one to hear me.

In the next instant I wanted to be back aboard *Galadriel*, to cast aside her winter raincover, and to go sailing

———

Not very many days later I was given another gift, the first tentative stirrings of a new friendship. I think it was Mary's attractive appearance of outdoor hardiness and her air of quiet self-sufficiency that caught my attention. Surprisingly, although her sailing experience was still limited, she had already begun to cruise alone in her own boat, a Cal-20 sloop only a few inches different in size from my own tiny cruiser.

Our paths seemed to cross with increasing frequency, on the dock, on the water, and in the unfrequented nook-and-cranny anchorages that we both seemed to favor among the islands. Like me, she appeared to be a real loner; already she had discovered the joys (and the occasional perils) of solo sailing.

From a basis of common interest and experience we cautiously moved toward a fondness for each other. It was something to which I might not have been open if that November afternoon of quiet island magic had not cracked the shell of my paralysis.

The hiatus in my life seemed at an end, and at last I was once again ready to spread my canvas to the wind.

# Mary Comes Aboard

 "When spring comes, why don't the two of us do a cruise in company?"

Mary was perched on her galley seat with a chart spread over her knees as she proposed this. I glanced at her chart; it showed some part of the coast far north of Oak Bay, where our boats lay alongside the dock under a light dusting of early winter snow. I craned my neck for a closer look. The narrow, winding strait upon which her finger lay appeared to be somewhere north of Desolation Sound.

"What destination do you have in mind?"

"Oh, nowhere in particular." Mary turned toward me with her enigmatic smile. "Just so long as it's a good long cruise up the coast."

I felt like jumping at the idea, but I had a doubt. I had grown very fond of Mary and knew I would enjoy sailing anywhere with her. But I was unsure of her experience. To sail a few hundred miles northward in a big ocean cruiser might be a relatively easy passage. In tiny craft like ours, however, little sailboats with waterline lengths of only about sixteen feet, a voyage like that would be harder work. I wondered if Mary realized how much harder.

"Summer's a long way off," I hedged. "Why don't we do something simpler right now?"

"Sure," said Mary, always enthusiastic for anything.

Here was my plan: Mary could come with me aboard *Galadriel* for a couple of days' hop over to a sheltered anchorage on nearby Discovery Island. Another of those incredible winter highs had just begun to shift onto the coast, and the next twenty-four hours at least would be sunny and warmer. We would make it brief, however; the cold, wet gales of December would not be held at bay forever.

Mary was thrilled at the prospect of her first cruise aboard my doughty old boat. Late in the afternoon, stocked up with tinned foods, coffee, and a good supply of fuel for the cabin heater, we raised the tan-bark mainsail and cast off the dock lines.

Although the temperature had risen dramatically, turning the brief final hours of the winter afternoon into mild spring, the wind was quite boisterous. It was a westerly, however, and forecast to stay in that quarter. This would mean a fast, easy run across to Discovery and a safe lee in the shallow northern cove where I planned to anchor for the night.

"I'll show you the advantage of *Galadriel*'s shoal-draft

design," I said to Mary. "We'll sail her right into the shallows of a creek mouth that most boats can't get into."

Mary took my pocket cruiser's helm, revealing at once her steering sensitivity. Even sailing very fast on the crests of a lumpy following sea, it was as if she had handled my boat a hundred times before. I watched the press of canvas swelling taut before the near-gale. As we flew along, the old thrill trembled back into my soul.

We hurtled toward the foamy westward shore of Discovery. As we approached, I took the helm. "The entrance to the passage between the islands is tricky," I explained, "especially when we're being shot toward it with a strong following wind."

It was a narrow, shallow gap toward which we were being flung. I hoped I could steer *Galadriel* into it without hitting anything. Mary, fully understanding the riskiness of our approach, seemed nevertheless to be sharing the excitement that I felt.

"I'd never dream of trying to get through that passage!"

"Smart woman! You're a better skipper than I am."

But we made it. In a welter of tumbling surf and with jagged rocks flashing past on either side, we slid through the channel's tricky dogleg to round up suddenly on the calm, sheltered mudflats where I intended to anchor. Under the lee of high bluffs and giant firs on Discovery's north side, no vestige of the gale penetrated. Revelling in the peace and quiet, we dropped the hook.

Mary was enchanted by the place. Even in the hour that

remained before the early winter sunset, the rays of light pouring between the trees carried a gratifying preview of spring's coming warmth. In the comfortable twilight we walked among the big trees, whose tops swayed before the blast from the west.

Rowing back to *Galadriel*, I assured Mary: "In a westerly like this, there's no snugger anchorage on the coast."

Had I forgotten the contemptuous line Hilaire Belloc once wrote about fools who suppose the wind cannot change its direction?

———

After a bubbling hot stew and a leisurely pastry with coffee, we burrowed into our sleeping bags. Our snug cove was a motionless mirror, and we fell asleep easily.

But we awoke an hour later, sensing that something had changed. Wavelets scrunched noisily against the boat's stem, and our bunks rose and fell with a jerky motion.

I opened the hatch to poke my head out into the night air that was suddenly breathtakingly cold. At first I could not believe my eyes, but reality quickly forced itself upon my sleepy brain. The wind had backed a full 180 degrees; it was now a northerly, and we were being pressed toward a shore on which surf was already exploding luminously in the darkness.

Below in the cabin, Mary had her ear pressed to the weather radio. "Oh dear!"

"What?"

"Bad! They've suddenly revised tonight's forecast. There's an arctic front pouring off the mainland. They're saying we'll have a storm-force northeaster."

Bad, she had said. It was worse than bad. In our shallow, north-facing cove with an arctic storm front rushing southward toward us, we were doomed!

Quickly struggling into my quilted cruiser suit, I leapt into the dinghy. Mary, now also in her bright orange storm suit, lowered our spare anchor and its chain carefully into the rocking, bouncing boat. I strained at the oars, pulling against a wind and chop that were already too much for me. I strained, and inch by inch I towed the second anchor cable to windward. Somewhere out there in the darkness I judged that I'd carried it far enough. When I had dropped the anchor, Mary hauled on the cable to drag the chain out straight and to feel the anchor-flukes bite into the sand-mud bottom.

"She's hooked bloody good!" Mary yelled. It was my first discovery of one of Mary's seagoing characteristics: in a crisis her grammar fails.

Within half an hour the wind was whistling at thirty-five knots. In another half hour it had risen to a howling forty, driving whitecrested ridges under our pitching vessel and ashore to break frighteningly on the rocky ledge that lay just astern. We sat up in our bunks, fully zipped and buckled into our cruiser suits.

I sat rigid with anxiety. If our anchors dragged, we would be on the ledge in ten seconds. "We could lose old *Galadriel* tonight," I said.

Mary, peering aft through the companionway at the fluorescent white mayhem thirty yards inshore of us, was clearly asking herself the same question that was passing through my mind: if the boat grounded and broke up in the surf on that ledge, how likely would it be that we could scramble ashore alive? Yet, with this grim reality in the offing, she lay back and closed her eyes.

At midnight the storm was literally screaming through our rigging. The stainless steel shrouds vibrated until I feared the old boat would be shaken apart by her own stays. We rose and fell at express-elevator speed on crests and into troughs. A grim voice on the weather channel reported that the Sea Bird Point lighthouse — only half a mile along the Discovery shore from our position — was now measuring fifty knots with higher gusts.

"Incredible!" Mary exclaimed, without opening her eyes. "And yet it appears that our anchors are still holding."

When I climbed out into the cockpit a few minutes later to give our cables more scope, Mary stood in the hatchway keeping a watch on my movements. The air was unbelievably frigid. At midafternoon we had fooled ourselves that we were in the tropics; this new arctic front had plunged us back to subfreezing levels. My first step over the cockpit coaming onto the deck brought a frightening revelation. A skin of black ice had turned the narrow side-decks into a skating rink.

Somehow I made my way forward and checked the angles of our anchor lines. Their thrumming, bar-taut tension made any attempt at paying out a few meters more scope an utter impossibility. I inched my way back to the cockpit, expecting each violent lurch of the deck to set me sliding over the side into the churning darkness.

Back in the relative security of the companionway I found that I was almost catatonic with fear. It was the arctic cold that I feared; its menace shattered my confidence more than the force of the gale.

"We'll sleep in our survival suits," Mary said.

"Sleep?" I queried unbelievingly.

Mary laughed (she actually laughed!). "Well ... doze, anyway. We can't do anything more. If the anchors let go, we'll wake up like a shot."

A few minutes later, as I squinted through the porthole beside my bunk to glimpse the crests that foamed past at deck level, I heard a distinct snore from the opposite bunk.

———

At dawn we were still alive. *Galadriel*'s two hooks had not dragged, but incredibly had held her precisely where she had been when the storm first swung her around. And a miracle was in progress; the wind was dropping as if someone were turning a control knob.

We struggled for an hour to break out the anchors, which had buried themselves halfway to China. But we did not do this before Mary had heated coffee and dished up bowls of muesli. This was another discovery about my new sailing-mate's seagoing character: she lets nobody get underway before they've fortified themselves with "a proper breakfast."

Eventually we sailed, punching our way homeward against a wind that was still powerful enough to necessitate a deep reef in the mainsail. As we crashed along through the icy swells left over from the storm, Mary stated that it had been a wonderfully exciting night.

Back at the dock we furled the sails with frostbitten fingers and stowed all the gear that had come adrift from lockers below.

Aboard Mary's boat an hour later, greatly calmed and warmed by the mug of steaming coffee that she had thrust into my hands, I pulled from its rack on the bulkhead the chart she had been studying the day before. She held one edge of the chart on her knee while I unrolled it and laid the opposite edge on my own.

Again her finger began to trace a winding passage from the northern reaches of the Strait of Georgia to a destination somewhere beyond.

"Right," I said. "When spring comes, let's drift northwards together."

In a private corner of my mind I hoped I'd be able to keep up with her.

$Countdown$

Spring arrived and very rapidly blossomed into a fine early summer. One day after work I sought out Mary to bring her some news. I found her on the dock alongside her boat *Aiaia*, kneeling among the white mounds of a sail on which she was doing some repair stitching.

After listening delightedly to my news, she exclaimed, "Two months! That's better than you hoped for. With two months' leave, we can really get somewhere."

It was true. With most of the summer and a couple of early autumn weeks available, we would have time to drift northwards into waters we had not previously explored. And we needed all the free time I had been able to get; little cruising boats are not fast passagemakers. I knew from much past experience that *Galadriel*, although capable of sprinting at six knots or more, will tend to average only about three over a long haul, coping with the vagaries of wind and tide.

Three knots, however, is fast enough for an exploration of paradise.

In her cabin Mary placed a pot of water on the stove for coffee. While it heated she spread charts on the bunk once again. We gazed at the labyrinth of channels and islands that sprawled for hundreds of miles up the inland sea between Vancouver Island and the British Columbia mainland.

For twenty-five years my sailing philosophy had strongly avoided the naming of specific goals. I had always let wind and tide decide my course and destination. But I surprised myself by saying to Mary, "Let's aim for Bute Inlet."

Straggling idly up the coast, we might not make it as far as Bute. In the attempt, however, we would stumble upon a thousand lovely places and memorable adventures.

Mary had pulled Bill Wolferstan's *Cruising Guide* from her bookshelf and had opened it to the chapter on the big northern fjords. The color photos showed deep, cold inlets walled by glaciated mountains. Mary noted that the advice to cruising sailors was a bit daunting. "Big outflow winds funnel down Bute Inlet," she said. "And anchorage in Bute is tricky; the place seems almost bottomless, hundreds of feet deep right up against shores that are practically vertical."

I watched, puzzled, as she quickly jotted something in her notebook. I asked what the little coil binder was.

"It's my supply list. I'm writing myself a reminder to buy a few hundred meters of extra anchor line."

The weeks that remained before our departure were filled with detailed planning and intense activity. At a sailors' secondhand warehouse we bought heavier chain, larger anchors and two months' supply of kerosene for stoves and lamps. We acquired expensive piles of new charts — in duplicate, to provide a set for each of the two boats. Cartons of food were gathered, and not just the tinned beans or stew that had traditionally been my cruising fare. Mary laid in a stock of onions, potatoes, pasta and rice for "proper meals."

Our preparation even included the building of a new dinghy. Through a mysterious chain of circumstances, *Aiaia*'s old fiberglass tender had gone missing, so I sketched a plan for something we could knock together quickly but neatly from plywood. During a long weekend of frenetically focused labor we created what we subsequently called "the twenty-four-hour dinghy." In optimistic contrast to its hasty birth, Mary named her new tender *Aie*, the classical Greek word that means "lasting forever."

As our little boats settled lower in the water under their weight of cruising stores and gear, our expectations soared. We could hardly contain our impatience to be under way. We believed that nothing could stop us now.

But a shocking turn of events aboard *Galadriel* almost did bring us to a full stop.

Not many days before the start of my leave, I did a quick daysail across to the Chatham Islands. Even loaded as she was, my boat danced lightly over the waves; she and

I were enjoying ourselves as always. The return was a moderately stiff bash against wind and swells that bounced us merrily and drenched the foot of the headsail with spray.

Half a mile from home I left the tiller for a moment to go below for a handful of trail mix and a sip of water. As I sat down to open a drawer, my eye fell on a bilge area that was visible through an opening beneath the galley locker. Although I had come below for water, the water that I saw in that bilge was far more than I really wanted. My pulse quickened with alarm as I realized that the boat's deep regions were awash in a tide of rusty water — gallons of the stuff!

Readers of my book about *Galadriel*'s early days will remember the chapters about her building. They will perhaps recall the painstaking efforts that I undertook to fit and fasten the iron-weighted bilge keels. Those keels were rigidly attached with very substantial bolts.

That careful assembly, however, was a long time past; those fine old keelbolts were now a quarter-century old.

As I stared in horror at the rising tide of seawater below the floorboards, I had fairly certain suspicions of its source. The blood-red stream of rust that was pouring in around a couple of the bolts seemed to confirm my diagnosis. I returned to the helm and sailed with all possible haste toward my berth in the marina. At intervals I peered below; the floodwaters down there were now swirling over the galley carpet.

*Galadriel* was slowly filling. Eventually she might actually sink!

When I was at last approaching the marina, I realized that there would be no point in rounding up and tying the boat alongside the dock. I couldn't leave her afloat, continuing to fill and settle lower, hour by hour, until perhaps she went under. Instead I threw the helm over and sailed her straight for the beach.

Ironically the dear old boat sailed beautifully and handled as nimbly as ever while she skimmed the shallows along the beach. I threw the helm again and she spun daintily shoreward, to ground on the gravelly slope immediately beside the boatyard's marine ways.

A wave of relief swept over me with the realization that I had put her safely ashore. But as I sat in the cockpit breathing a grateful sigh, another emotion overwhelmed me; I felt a cold chill of despair. Keelbolts — especially long, very rusted, iron bolts — are the very devil to withdraw from old hardwood keels and iron castings. Their replacement is a process of major surgery.

The thought crossed my mind that my beloved *Galadriel* was finished.

———

The following day, hauled out onto the ways, the boat drained rapidly, sad rivulets of brownish seawater dribbling out of gaps between keel and hull in the vicinity of at least two major keelbolts. Mary, typically, did not share my pessimism; instead she urged me to quickly get under way with repairs.

"We're due to sail in just three days!" I groaned. "I don't think it can be done."

As Boatworks shipwright Rick studied the situation long and hard, his face betrayed the same sentiment. Nevertheless he got started at once with the struggle to draw the old bolts.

After a day's pounding, drilling, wrenching — and cursing — he got the three especially corroded bolts out. In dismay we stared at them, lying on the gravel underneath the boat. When I had installed these two-foot-long galvanized iron bolts a quarter-century earlier, they were a robust half-inch in diameter. Now the corroded remains narrowed at certain points to only about an eighth of an inch.

How glad I was to have discovered this perilous situation before setting out on a two-month voyage!

Throughout another long day Rick worked on my keels, fitting new bolts of stainless steel bedded in one of the new high-tech sealants. When he did the final cinching of the nuts, seated on large steel washers, sealant jetted out of the offending gaps between hull and keels. "That's done it!" he proudly announced. "There'll be no more leakage now, and these keels won't be falling off, I can guarantee."

At high water late in the afternoon we refloated *Galadriel*. Not a drop of water seeped into the bilge, which remained dust-dry even after I had kept watch on the bolt-tops for an hour or more. Overjoyed, I hugged Mary, I hugged Rick, I kissed the deck of the beloved boat.

Only one day now remained before our planned departure.

# Gulf Islands Beginning

Scarcely a ripple of wake trailed astern as my boat ghosted up Haro Strait in the noonday heat. A few hundred yards away on a parallel course, Mary seemed virtually motionless on the water, her big, candy-striped, lightweather headsail barely lifting in the zephyr of following breeze.

We were on our way.

At this rate our drift up Haro Strait might appear to be like an attempt to walk to the moon. We had started, however, with a hidden asset. My co-workers always chuckle at me when I'm planning my vacations; asked to choose my holiday-time I invariably tell them that, before committing myself to specific dates, I first have to consult the tidebook.

For the start of this trip, as always, I had selected a day that favored us with a long, all-afternoon flood. We reclined at our tillers, unconcerned by the summery stillness, for we were riding a tidal conveyor belt that would carry us up to the nearest of the Gulf Islands, wind or no wind.

I was pretty sure that we would arrive somewhere by the end of the day, perhaps even at a destination that I was secretly hoping for, as our first night's anchorage. Of course we could give ourselves a boost; we both had outboard auxiliaries for this trip. They were minimalist engines, however, with very strictly limited supplies of fuel. Our cruise would be accomplished primarily by sail, using wind and current to best advantage and saving the outboards only for circumstances in which the kindly spirits truly deserted us.

Late in the day, after we had been carried very slowly northward for almost eight hours, we had my secret destination in sight a mile or two ahead. The place was a low-lying, minuscule islet whose projecting arms of rock I knew embraced an unseen cubbyhole for small craft in good weather. It was a place I wanted Mary to see. And we had the first real breeze of the day, a light but steady southwesterly that propelled us in just the right direction.

Mary gently eased her *Aiaia* alongside *Galadriel*. "You seem to know where you're going, but ..."

"Let's anchor there," I said, pointing. "It's Reay Island, a special place."

Mary's brow wrinkled in puzzlement. "Do you mean that little knob just ahead? But it's not an island, it's just a rockpile!"

In response to my rather coy "wait-and-see" answer she fell a boat-length or two astern and let me lead the way.

As we approached the dangerous-looking row of stone turrets that curved outward from the main islet, *Aiaia* seemed to hang back even more cautiously. When I had sailed around into their jagged embrace, however, Mary followed, to make the discovery that I had hoped she would enjoy — a microscopically tiny anchorage that shoaled into a wedge of sand at its head.

The Reay Island anchorage is a tight squeeze — and doubtful shelter — for just one anchored boat of even *Galadriel*'s size. Somehow we managed to find a way to jigsaw both of us into the space, each with a pair of anchors to provide the illusion of security.

Taking to the dinghies, we explored the sculptured sandstone galleries and sandy shallows along the island's fringes. In the warm red glow of sunset we walked the grassy meadow atop this wildflower-strewn mesa and sat on the precarious pinnacles of its adjacent turrets for an aerial view of our boats as they lay beneath our feet. When darkness fell we toasted marshmallows over a twig fire on the beach below the tideline. By the time we rowed out to spend the night together aboard *Aiaia*, Mary's skepticism about the unpromising rockpile of Reay Island had completely disappeared.

———

Two subsequent days' sailing turned out to be similar to our first. In the lightest of breezes we used the afternoon floods to carry us slowly on our way.

Our second night's anchorage, in Prevost Island's big, pondlike Annette Inlet, was warm and quiet. Aboard *Aiaia* that evening Mary demonstrated her style of shipboard cookery on a one-burner galley stove. Not inspired by my usual tinned hash or beans, she grated fresh spuds and onions for a treat that was new to me — potato pancakes fried in butter and served with sour cream and applesauce.

We idled northward from Prevost against a weak morning ebb, hoping to reach the rather tricky tidal channel of Porlier Pass at low-water slack, and then to catch the flood in the Strait of Georgia.

In more than twenty years of pottering about under sail, I had always been content to let these southern Gulf Islands be the whole of my cruising world. I had found deep satisfaction in the meditative stillness of these little waters and the unfrequented nooks and notches that they offer to a shoal-draft boat like *Galadriel*. Now, if we could make our way through Porlier Pass at the slack, we would be "outside" and on our way up the Strait of Georgia. We would leave astern, after our couple of days' sailing, the realm that I had been content to explore for decades.

Trincomali Cannel was calm and hot. Running slowly up the long corridor between Salt Spring and Galiano islands, we might easily have imagined ourselves to be in Baja California; one almost expected to see tall saguaro cactus on the dry, brown hillsides.

Under the swelling balloon of her red-and-white lightweather jib, Mary's boat crept slowly ahead of mine, gradually putting each of us into our own quiet solitude as we drifted along. With a trickle of ebb against us we made slow progress. But we were moving; I watched Mary, half a mile ahead of me, creep up alongside Wallace Island's southern headland. Although it seemed an eternity before I whispered my way up to that point, a brief catspaw of breeze that suddenly filled my sails allowed me to catch up with *Aiaia* about halfway along the island's long, straight, eastern shore.

In the utterly windless calm that followed I saw Mary drop and lash down her headsail, our usual sign to each other that we're going to give up and do a bit of motoring. Dropping my jib, I fired up the two-horsepower Honda outboard on my sternbracket. Most sailing folks eye my toy engine with distrust. After years of engineless cruising, however (using a long oar as my auxiliary power), I now find the four-knot speed imparted by my tiny Honda quite breathtaking.

Side by side we buzzed along over the mirror-flat sea. Motoring in that calm was like an episode from *Lawrence of Arabia*; the motionless air was an oven under the unrelenting eye of a blazing sun. Mary gestured at me and over the unaccustomed clamor of our engines yelled an urgent message that I could not understand. Then it sank in: pointing to her own head and then repeatedly toward mine, she was urging me to put on my forgotten sunhat. As I drew its shady brim over my eyes I realized that the headache I had begun to develop was not solely due to my hatred of outboard motors.

Thanks to those poor maligned machines we arrived at

the entrance of Porlier Pass just at slack water.

The timing was important, because the nine-knot tidal race through the pass produces chaotic turbulence for small craft attempting to sail through. Now, with scarcely a ripple on its flat surface, Porlier Pass let us through in ten easy minutes.

As we passed the light on Race Point, wind arrived. After quickly munching a tin of smoked herring, my first snack in many hours, I raised sail. Mary was already off up the Strait of Georgia with her big genoa filling purposefully.

Aided now by the beginning of the flood, we ran up Valdes Island's eight-mile-long eastern coastline, the blue expanse of wide Strait of Georgia spreading away into the haze on our starboard side. Out here on this strait I felt that we were really on our way north.

When the afternoon ended, we entered Commodore Passsage, among the Flat Top Islands. In the innermost reaches of that cluster a throng of yachts lay at anchor in busy Silva Bay. We did not sail that far in; our anchorage for the night was a hidden gap between two of the smaller outer islands, a snug privacy for pocket cruisers like ours.

We had come to the end of the familiar region of short passages and sheltered waters. Tomorrow we would set out on our first really big hop into open space. Peering out through gaps between our sheltering isles at the evening-misted breadth of the strait, we began to see our sixteen-foot-waterline boats from a newly dawning perspective. All at once they seemed even smaller.

After one of Mary's typical cruising suppers, a luscious

Swiss-chard omelette with hot panfried bread, we listened to the weather radio.

"Perfect!" Mary exclaimed. "A strong southeasterly for our first big run up the strait."

# A Backward Glance

Our first three days had been typical Gulf Islands sailing — hot, windless, and slow. At dawn in the Flat Tops we awoke to something different.

The anchor lines lay out taut and our rigging hummed in the twenty-five-knot wind that pressed in from the southeast. Out beyond the protection of the islands, large whitecapped swells marched up the strait. Over our breakfast of hot nine-grain cereal and coffee I asked Mary if she was worried by the conditions out there in the open water.

"Sure," she admitted. "But we prayed for wind, and we've got it. We're sure as hell not going to sit here and waste it!"

After breakfast we brought our anchors up. I watched with a trace of apprehension as Mary strained to haul her boat forward against the wind and to lift on deck the over-size cruising hook that she had used since our scary winter night at Discovery Island.

As soon as we got underway, the stiff following wind carried us very swiftly through the narrow gap between Lily and Vance islands, into the tumble of large crests out-side. A few miles northward, beyond the sheltering lee of the islands, we discovered the conditions in which our day's run up the Strait of Georgia would be sailed.

I watched, fascinated, as *Aiaia* surfed ahead, rising onto high toppling ridges and disappearing into deep troughs. *Galadriel* must have presented a similar spectacle from Mary's perspective. The ninety-mile open-water fetch from Puget Sound up to Lasqueti Island gives this strait an open-sea feeling in a brisk southerly wind.

———

As we began our run, I recalled my previous summer's ex-perience of a real open-sea passage. The events of that wild sailing trip gave a perspective with which to compare to-day's somewhat daunting sea-state.

Planning a lone voyage to Mexico aboard his fifteen-ton cutter *Sine Timore*, my friend Iwo had looked around for somebody to share the first leg of the voyage, the noto-rious Victoria-to-San Francisco passage. I jumped at the opportunity and agreed to join him as crew.

After passing Cape Flattery and heading out into the Pacific, we set a course that would keep us prudently offshore. At the outermost point of our long southward curve we would be about 120 miles out to sea from the US west coast.

The voyage turned out to be one of the greatest sailing experiences of my life, but it included some interesting revelations about the differences between Gulf Islands pottering and offshore passagemaking. Two aspects of the adventure turned out to be extraordinarily strange.

For two days after we left Cape Flattery astern we ran before a light northerly breeze in southsea conditions. I revelled in my first days ever of sailing beyond sight of land, on an ocean that lived up to its Pacific name — in temporary contrast to its reputation at this latitude on this coast. Iwo had a hunch that this would be a gentler run than he had expected. Soon, however, the normal September weather pattern off the Oregon coast reestablished itself — and did so with a vengeance.

During our third night out we found wind and sea rising dramatically. The two of us exchanged worried glances as we listened to the marine forecast: a storm-force northwester with accompanying heavy seas. By the time the wind had reached gale force, we had already furled all of *Sine Timore*'s canvas except a tiny storm staysail, and we had streamed a drogue over the stern on the end of six hundred feet of heavy warp to try to hold the ship's stern square to the big following seas.

Under her little scrap of sail and towing the drogue, the vessel continued to run fast. In the early hours of morning we learned from the marine broadcast that the sea in our vicinity was intensifying, with swell heights of twenty feet. To keep her safe as she surfed along in these conditions, we steered continuously, each of us taking the helm for a couple of hours while the other slept below. As the seas built higher, our southward sleighride became progressively wilder. I found that I loved my watches at the wheel; this was rare fun!

It was during my hours alone at the helm that I had my two interesting experiences.

During one of my daylight watches, concentrating intently on my continuous battle to keep the ship on course and safely stern-to in the breaking crests that thunderously overtook us, I became dimly aware of something odd. All around me, from the corner of my eye, I caught glimpses of islands. If I did not look up from the steering compass, my impression of the islands became stronger. To starboard lay a distinct, Galiano-shaped ridge; over the rail to port I could sense the high dome of a Salt Spring.

Yet we were 120 miles offshore. The nearest land of any kind lay far beyond the horizon. When I looked up, I saw nothing but a tumbling emptiness of ocean, heaving and spuming its way to the horizon in every direction. When I fixed my eye on the compass again for a while, the islands were back, surrounding the ship as she bounded along.

Clearly, after my decades of inshore pottering, I had the Gulf Islands permanently branded into my brain.

The lone night watches were even more enchanting, but they too held a strange spell in store for me. I thrilled to the unaccustomed fascination of being alone on deck, while Iwo slept below, as the cutter raced down the luminous faces of big following seas in the eerie silver light of a full moon. The continuous struggle with the helm to avoid broaching on the steep wavefronts was exhilarating. The moonlit crests that mounted to the rail and spilled onto *Sine Timore*'s deck as they foamed past thrilled me with their dangerous beauty.

It was during these surrealistic night watches that I enjoyed the second odd manifestation. I began to hear music. In the rhythmic surge and roar of the overtaking seas and in the pulsing tympany of the ship's curling bow wave I heard a choir. As the hours passed, the ethereal song became increasingly elaborate, a great choral work sung by five hundred voices.

The moon gleamed coldly down on the tumultuous ocean; down its unearthly silver path the ship surfed southward, barely held in control by my trembling fist on the helm. All the while the music swelled about me, so vivid and original in its details that a Mozart might have transcribed it and presented the composition as one of his own great works.

At one moment the music was suddenly squelched. A ton of bricks avalanched against my back, flinging me headlong onto my face and skidding me forward in the cockpit until the lifeline attached to my safety harness brought me up short. When I struggled to my feet I was knee deep in seawater that had just begun to drain through the scuppers. As Iwo sprang on deck to see if I was still aboard, the breaking crest that had pooped us was still rolling away

ahead of us in the moonlight.

During one of the skipper's watches, while I slept below (on the cabin sole, under the table), we broached heavily. With a clamorous bang the yacht lurched over onto her beam-ends, knocked down under a whelm of heavy seawater. Now it was my turn to leap on deck, afraid of finding Iwo gone, leaving the frayed end of his lifeline still attached to its ringbolt in the cockpit.

When we stood together surveying the wild night scene, I heard it again, the surpassingly lovely and awesomely profound nocturnal oratorio. It was very strange!

Our approach to the Golden Gate was a breakneck toboggan-ride on huge shoreward-rushing swells. We shot under the storybook bridge and, inside, we finally slipped into stillness. Alongside a wharf at San Francisco's public marina Iwo and I grinned at each other and shook hands.

I had discovered that running in big seas was fine sport — at least in a fifteen-ton cutter.

Just such a run, although in narrower waters and in less than a full gale, was what Mary and I were embarking upon, with the forty-mile-distant smudge of Lasqueti on the horizon as our goal.

# A Shimmer on the Horizon

 A sailing passage of thirty or forty nautical miles in a fifteen-ton yacht is likely to be pretty quick and easy. In a featherweight pocket cruiser the same trip is a rather different experience; it will typically be far more labor-intensive.

As we tumbled past Protection Island, running north before our bracing morning southeaster, we began to feel what was in store for us. The essential feature of small-craft cruising is motion — quick, unpredictable, violent, bruising motion. Bracing myself continually against my boat's prancing, bucking attempts to fling me overboard, I felt muscles everywhere in my body starting to ache before we had sailed five miles.

Mary, already quite far ahead, was an instructive sight. As always, my view of her boat staggering among the curling ridges gave a more accurate impression of the sea's chaotic state than the sensation of my own motion did. At times *Aiaia* was a flash of white balancing on a watery summit; at other moments she was eclipsed in the trough, showing only her top-rigging above a fence of foam.

Once I snapped up a pair of binoculars and managed to raise them to my eyes long enough for a close glance at Mary. In that instant she was steering with one hand and using the other hand to raise a thermos flask to her lips.

Northward up the Strait of Georgia an almost imaginary mountaintop showed a vague shimmer of itself above a hard, blue horizon. Chart and compass confirmed that this was Lasqueti Island, a possible destination for us today if our favoring wind held. The nearest point of the island was over thirty-five miles from our morning's starting place among the Flat Tops.

Our real sailing distance would be much longer, thanks to Whiskey Golf. Straddling the direct course between Entrance Island and Lasqueti, Whiskey Golf is a huge wedge of the Strait of Georgia that has been designated a naval weapons testing range. When this military zone is active (on all weekdays), marine traffic must avoid it altogether. Thus our course for the day would be the two long sides of a right angle, close inshore as far as the Ballenas Islands, then eastward to our goal on Lasqueti.

Tossed and buffeted in a rough sea, we would find this a long and exhausting run. Yet on the threshold of such a run there is something that we fear more than strengthening wind and a roughening sea: it is far more troublesome

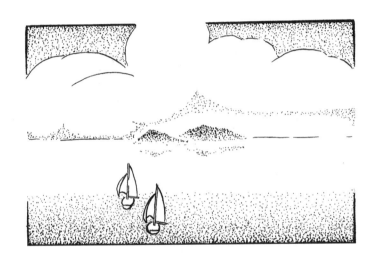

for us to discover, miles from our destination, that the wind has suddenly stopped. Our boats are wind-driven ships; we don't try to push them far by outboard power.

Mary was exhilarated by her first crossing of big open water. This I could tell by the style of her sailing. Spreading a sizeable area of canvas wing-on-wing, she was letting *Aiaia* have her head, running much faster than old *Galadriel* could manage. Quickly she shrank to little more than a triangular white dot far ahead.

And then she sailed back!

Rising and falling precariously alongside, she gave me an optimistic thumbs-up sign. Then with a throw of her helm she was off again, enjoying the sport of surfing at hull-speed-plus on the slopes of the northward-marching waves.

We galloped along our way for several hours, with the wind holding steady at about twenty-five knots. *Galadriel* sailed as all short-waterline cruising boats tend to do, rocketing forward at breakneck speed on the crests and wallowing at times to a near stop in the troughs. It is this feature of a very small vessel's heavy weather performance that gives rise to a paradox: some superfast sailing is combined with a slower-than-expected overall passage speed. Thirty-five miles of this good fun is hard work!

Although it is difficult for a lone sailor to leave the helm while the boat is corkscrewing over the waves under a press of canvas, sometimes it must be done. When need arises one may heave-to by rounding up into the wind, leaving the headsail sheeted on the windward side to fill in reverse, against the mainsail's forward thrust. This stops the vessel's forward motion but not, of course, her rise and fall on the seas. Getting lunch or using the head in such conditions is like attempting these functions inside an automatic washing machine. When I returned on deck after heaving-to for five minutes, I found that I was displaying a spectacular scrape on my arm, a souvenir of my collision with a drawer in the cabin. Half a mile ahead, *Aiaia* too was momentarily stopped, lying over at a high angle of heel. I kept a prudent watch until Mary re-emerged and cast off her jibsheet to resume sailing.

We ran on. As the afternoon advanced, the hedgehog profile of the southernmost of the Ballenas Islands loomed directly ahead, and the mountains of Lasqueti began to solidify out of the haze. I was starting to feel very weary, but the thrill of our rushing progress continued. Although both Mary and I were carrying headsails too large for the press of wind and swell, the risk seemed justified by our gratifying speed.

During a later day's run on this summer voyage I would learn a lesson about the danger of breakneck surfing in the Strait of Georgia.

It was suppertime when we drew abreast of the Ballenas Islands. Boat Cove, on Lasqueti's south shore, lay only about eight miles ahead; it was a tantalizing goal as an end to our long day's run. We faced a problem, however: after our many hours of boisterous, steady wind, a typical summer evening calm had suddenly begun to settle around us.

We drew abreast of each other to share a snack and to

confer. "Boat Cove looks like a possibility," Mary said.

"I don't know. It's getting late, and we're losing the wind. Shall we call it a day here and anchor between the Ballenas Islands?"

"I can actually see the entrance to Boat Cove in the haze over there. Let's go for it!"

The final eight miles were an increasingly slow drift. As the sun dropped to the horizon, we lowered sail for an engine-powered push along the steep shore of Sangster Island, whose high, narrow spine was like an arrow pointing directly to the mouth of our intended anchorage.

When we entered Boat Cove at last, dusk was gathering around us. At the head of that big, quiet inlet we found shallows in which, after a couple of failed attempts to make our anchors set securely, we eventually got ourselves safely hooked. Both of us sat on deck, exhausted but gazing happily at the steeply sloping fields and deep woods that lay about us. Although open to the south — the direction from which the wind had blown all day — the cove was comfortable enough in the profound calm that had settled in for the night.

For once Mary was too exhausted to insist on any culinary refinements. Without complaint she settled for the tin of stew that I heated over *Galadriel*'s primus stove. We had arrived at Lasqueti, where during days that followed we would discover an especially mesmerizing vision of the island dream.

# Where It's Always Afternoon

We were awake at dawn and were raising our anchors not long afterward. When the day's wind began to build from the south, we would find Boat Cove less safe and comfortable than it had been during the gloriously still night.

Our aim was to sail around the northwest end of the island and down into Scottie Bay, where we would stay for a day or two to explore Lasqueti. We little expected the spell that the place would cast upon us. On this bright morning, pausing briefly on our northward run, we would have been surprised had we foreseen how the island's enchantment was fated to make us lose all track of time.

By midmorning we were gliding among the Finnerties,

an intriguing maze of islands and channels on Lasqueti's upper corner. This gemlike mini-archipelago was probably first seen by European mariners as early as 1791, when Jose Maria Narvaez explored the Strait of Georgia aboard the Spanish schooner *Saturnina*. Oddly, the islands were not officially named until mid-twentieth century, when they and the adjacent Fegan Group were given names that honored a prominent World War II casualty, Captain "Finnerty" Fegan.

Drifting through the group, with little isles close about us to port and starboard, we idled along their sheltered waterways under the hot summer sun. Artfully designed cedar-shake cottages and miniature floathouses tucked into tiny coves gave this place a storybook character. We felt a yearning to linger there.

In fact, later we would be back among the Finnerty Islands to spend quiet evenings rowing our dinghies into their secret lagoons and backwaters. Today, however, we spread our sails to the breeze that had begun to rise from astern.

As we rounded the top of Lasqueti, we met the beginnings of the day's twenty-knot southeasterly wind. For the first time in several days we were no longer running before the wind but beating into it closehauled. Bracing myself against a sharp heeling angle and straining at the helm to drive *Galadriel* up into steep head-seas, I felt once again a certain qualm: our homeward passage against the prevailing southerly winds would be a long, arduous thrash. Later in the day, when I voiced this concern, Mary gave what was

to become her characteristic response: "Have faith! When we need to run south, we'll find winds that will serve."

Our progress around the top of Lasqueti was slow and wet with driven spray. Early in the afternoon, however, we had tacked our way down to a point at which we could free the sails and slide on an easy reach toward the entrance of Scottie Bay. On large, foaming swells we surfed toward the narrow gap. Beyond it we could glimpse a corner of Scottie Bay's marvellously sheltered lagoon dreaming quietly in its haze of warm sunshine. The look of the place, and our white-knuckled approach to its entrance, recalled a fragment of verse:

> *"Courage!" he said, and pointed toward the land,*
> *"This mounting wave will roll us shoreward soon."*
> *In the afternoon they came unto a land*
> *In which it seemèd always afternoon.*
> *All around the coast the languid air did swoon,*
> *Breathing like one that hath a weary dream.*

Through the narrow gap we sailed, carefully skirting an underwater ledge that half closed the passage, and found ourselves suddenly in the Lotus Land that Tennyson's lines described.

A few boats lay atop their reflections in the bay's deep outer basin. We drifted among them under sail, unwilling to break the uncanny silence by using our engines. We ghosted past, continuing into the shallower headwater of the anchorage, where, sheltered by the close embrace of high sandstone bluffs, we maneuvered very slowly toward a good stopping-place, our sails barely filling with any breeze at all. Finally we rafted together on a single anchor in a few feet of backwater quietude.

In this same place, many days later, we were to encounter a man who made me feel glad that, working our way into the anchorage under sail without engines, we had honored the special silence here.

———

Country roads. Quiet, unpaved tracks winding among majestic cedar and fir woods. These images stay with me from our many days of rambling on Lasqueti.

How many days (or weeks) in total did we remain there, held by this special island's fragrant, summery spell? Each morning on waking we speculated about whether this was the day to continue our voyage. The long, hot afternoon always found us strolling among the big trees, unable to focus on our speculative plans.

A major element of Lasqueti's fantasy environment was its people. Walking the forest roads we met people also walking. Time seemed to matter to these island folks as little as it had come to matter to us. People we encountered on the road — men, women and children — all stopped to talk. Standing or sitting for a while by the dusty roadside under the shade of giant cedars, they asked us where we were anchored, told us of places on the island we might visit, and invited us to coming events in which we might like to join.

When I commented happily on the lack of road traffic, a young woman explained that the absence of any car-ferry to Lasqueti is part of the island's charm. "Visitors have to arrive as foot-passengers or the way you two have come. They can't bring their cars!"

We began to discover that in a small island community people's dealings with each other are wonderfully different from such things ashore in the city. In a tidy forest clearing not far from Scottie Bay we happened upon an example. Tucked in among the great trees, a cottage-industry home sawmill lay beside its operator's cabin, surrounded by neat piles of sawn posts, studs and cedar boards. The place was deserted; no owner was in sight. But a notice on a shake-roofed signboard invited people to "help yourself to lumber. Leave your name on the notepad; we'll settle up sometime later."

A 1960s mood seemed alive and well on Lasqueti. Sitting almost every day in the sun on log-end benches at a vegetarian store and restaurant at False Bay, we enjoyed the island style of long, tie-dyed dresses, blue jeans and floppy straw sunhats.

Over a lazy supper there one evening we chatted with a man who joined us at our outdoor picnic table. Lanky, bearded and sunburned, he sat bouncing his year-old daughter on his knee. They lived in a cabin a few miles down the shore from Scottie Bay, he told us. We should up anchor and drift down to visit him sometime.

When Mary showed her liking for his baby girl, he said, "Look what she likes to do … " and, placing her feet carefully on the palm of his big open hand, he cautiously withdrew his other hand from its supporting position against her back. There she stood, balancing upright on his palm, smiling coyly while he talked and laughed with us.

To me the relaxed, happy stance of the balancing baby was a summation of the Lasqueti mood.

Strolling back along the road near sunset, we stopped at one of the "happenings" to which several of the islanders had invited us. On a grassy sward under the eaves of the forest a rustic band created bewitching music with flutes, guitars, and the resonant homebuilt marimbas that were a fad on the island that summer. Young dancers in long, cotton skirts swirled on the grass while we bystanders shared a food-laden table with an eager buzz of Lasqueti wasps.

Back aboard our rafted boats in Scottie Bay we wondered if we would ever break the spell and continue on our way. It began to seem unlikely.

On several perfect days we never ventured beyond the fifty-yard radius of the inner lagoon itself. We lay back on deck reading, we dozed in the sunshine, occasionally we watched an elegantly old-fashioned rowboat skim quietly across the bay. Life seemed more peaceful that summer in this snug, walled haven than it had been a half-century earlier. Much of the settlement and activity around this bay, described by Elda Copley Mason in her *Lasqueti Island History & Memory*, seemed to have receded and vanished, leaving Scottie Bay a quieter and more inactive backwater in the 1990s.

We lazed about on the smooth sandstone ledges that

fringed the lagoon, unmoving in the hot sunshine, while our rafted vessels dreamed on top of unruffled images of themselves. More days passed; we lost track of their number. Our only worry on water-short Lasqueti was the diminishing level of our drinking water tanks. In the endless string of dry, hot days we would soon have to give up washing, drinking or cooking with water.

Strangely, we could not stir ourselves to care about it.

*Lasqueti Garden*

 At least in the matter of our water shortage, Mary's "Have Faith" philosophy quickly proved itself.

When our supply had become so low as to shake our unconcerned poise, a sudden afternoon blackness darkened the western sky. Soon that black curtain began to be rent by lightning, and thunder rumbled across the anchorage to echo off the high sandstone bluffs.

From a locker somewhere in *Aiaia*'s bilge, Mary dug out a special piece of cruising gear that she had purchased for precisely this occasion. It was a large, clean tarpaulin of chemically inert synthetic material, perfect for gathering and funneling rainwater. While she industriously rigged her tarp to slope across her boat's cockpit toward waiting buckets, I made somewhat cruder catchment arrangements aboard *Galadriel*.

No sooner had we completed these preparations than the rain began. Down it spilled, tropical in its intensity. Through the evening, while a veritable monsoon splashed on the deck overhead, we prepared and enjoyed one of Mary's elaborate suppers — stir-fried vegetables, subtly seasoned and boiled new potatoes, with sliced ham fried in butter and a touch of maple syrup. Later, in the Cal-20's forepeak double berth, we were lulled to sleep by the hypnotic drumming of rain a few inches above our heads.

In the morning, which dawned clear and sunny again, we had fresh water by the bucketload. After filling all our containers with enough water for weeks, we bathed in fresh water and even washed clothing. Then we discovered that we had gallons more at our disposal, for our dinghies had filled with rainwater. Sometimes the natural environment, when it responds to one's need, seems to do so in a mood of amused excess.

As we continued spellbound in this congenial place, a healthy transformation occurred. By slow degrees the goal-oriented nature of this summer's voyage dissolved and vanished. Or at least it wavered sufficiently to permit some measure of my old cruising philosophy, which had always allowed me to feel unconcerned about not getting anywhere in particular.

Mary seemed content with our languorous days. We were delighted by the summer evenings, too, with their long, warm lucidity. Pottering in the protected shallows in our dinghies on several nights, we rediscovered the simple joy of rowing, as I had begun to do during my restorative winter crossing to Mary Tod Island many months before.

A typical evening's excursion, after our leisurely supper, included an idle drift along the sandstone ledges that skirted the anchorage, looking at colorful starfish in the tidal pools and watching pert kingfishers dive, with their shrill cry, to catch minnows.

When the sun had dipped below treetops to the west, we enjoyed a high-water passage through the shallow narrows between Lindberg Island and the Lasqueti shore. Drifting over the sandbar in that gap, we hung over the gunwales of the dinghies, captivated by the geometric perfection of sand dollars that carpeted the bottom, inches below our keels. Less than an arm's length down into the warm seawater we could push our fingers into the sand to pick up the dollars. To the present day an especially perfect Lasqueti sand dollar adorns the bulkhead over *Galadriel*'s galley stove.

Slipping through the gap as the long summer twilight settled luminously upon the water, we rowed a gentle circumnavigation of Lindberg Island. Its outer shores, with their wave-scalloped sandstone galleries and archways, were like a museum of surrealistic sculpture, strangely highlighted and shadowed in the soft, late-evening glow.

When we returned to bed, our anchored vessels were moonlit ghosts in the cool dusk.

After one twilight excursion we returned to find a truly fantastic shape looming in the darkness near our boats. The slender, exotic form, although slightly unbelievable at first glance, was unmistakable; she was *China Cloud*, the Chinese junk owned and sailed by the famous boatbuilder Allen Farrell.

I had actually met Allen Farrell a very long time ago. In about 1961, when he once invited me aboard his great seagoing schooner *Ocean Girl*, he seemed like an athletic youth, and I myself was scarcely more than a boy. Now, at age eighty, he was a legend; his elegant, handcrafted ships and his quiet, engineless style of cruising had made him an icon among sailing traditionalists.

Very late in the evening, when the long twilight had faded to darkness, I continued to stare across the water at the graceful apparition that lay anchored so close by.

The following day, on a baking-hot, flower-perfumed afternoon (it still seemed always afternoon), we walked up a trail that climbed the embankment alongside which our boats were rafted. A hundred yards back into the woods we found ourselves hiking beside a ramshackle fence that was fragrantly draped with a variety of flowering vines. At its end, where it took a right-angled turn to enclose a space within, the fence was interrupted by a tall, wire gate.

We might have passed by and continued on our way, but a small thing occurred that drew our attention. It was a shrill, wild cry from somewhere behind the fence.

Mary peered through the gate. "Look at this magnificent bird! It's a pileated woodpecker."

I glanced in over her shoulder. Clinging upright on the side of a tall fir spar was a very large and elegant bird, feathered in neat grey-brown but crested with bright scarlet. As we watched, it uttered its high call again and then

surveyed the space around itself with a proprietorial air. I looked away for a moment and when I turned my head again the bird was gone from its perch on the fir trunk.

Within the fenced area, under the shade of old fruit trees and taller forest cedars and firs that overhung its perimeter, lay a garden that looked peaceful and cool. Although it was generally a bit wild and unkempt, it included raised beds with neat rows of growing vegetables — salad crops, the big leaves of squash plants, even a tall stand of corn.

Suddenly a deep, gentle, woman's voice said, "Would you like to come inside? May I show you my garden?"

How had we failed to notice her at first? She stood under the shade of a tall flowering bush, a slender, young-ish woman in jeans and a smocked blouse, with her long hair bound in a red kerchief. In response to her gesture of welcome, we opened the gate.

Within its foliage-covered deer-fence the garden was a world unto itself. Proudly its owner walked us up and down among the recently watered beds of herbs and vigorously growing vegetables. A corner of the large space contained tubs of tomato plants, already heavy with their warmly red produce.

"Beautiful, isn't it?" the gardener said. "This property isn't mine; it belongs to somebody else. But I've planted my garden here every summer for years. It's becoming a lovelier, more mature garden all the time."

We agreed that it was a fine garden, and we marveled at this new manifestation of the island lifestyle. How extraordinary it seemed that someone could maintain an elaborate vegetable plantation year after year without having to own the land on which it all developed and matured. The geometrically arranged beds, nestling among borders of wilder growth, showed much loving care. Strolling among them with the young woman, we gained a favorable insight into her personality.

"I'm happy in my garden," she told us, quite unnecessarily.

As we prepared to leave, she filled our arms with Swiss chard, young onions, new potatoes, and a tomato or two. "I'll enjoy the thought of you two enjoying my fresh vegetables aboard your little boats down there in the bay."

And indeed, our evening stir-fry that night was the best ever!

———

I awoke in the dim, misty hour before dawn. We were still undecided whether at sunup this morning we would hoist anchor and at last resume our northward sail. For several minutes I gazed sleepily around the dusky bay.

Then my eye fell upon that morning's very special apparition. Like a half-materialized spectre in the haze, *China Cloud* was gliding slowly over the cove's unrippled glass surface. Although not the merest breath of a zephyr stirred, the phantom ship moved purposefully out toward the entrance. The sense of unreality was enhanced by the absence of sound; she was slipping away from the anchorage in utter silence. The ship's lean, whitehaired skipper himself seemed ethereal as he stood on the high stern deck plying the long yuloh, or Chinese oar, in graceful slow motion.

As the junk slid quietly out through the gap, I stood riveted, unwilling to break the silence even to call Mary, aboard her boat alongside mine, to witness the scene. Within a few minutes *China Cloud* was gone, had dematerialized into the haze outside the bay. Like most people when they have seen a ghost, I was left wondering if the ghost ship had existed at all.

When Mary awoke and I told her about the predawn departure that I had watched, she suddenly felt as I did. It was time for us to follow that ship out through the gap.

# Two Nights of Unease

We were in trouble!

Throughout a long day we had inched our way northward, borne very slowly by a light following breeze. Yet by early evening, when the haven we had optimistically hoped to reach was in sight close ahead, conditions changed suddenly. We began to realize that we were not going to make it.

We had snail-paced along to a position well beyond Texada Island's north end, and the low, sandy profile of Savary Island now seemed enticingly within reach over our bows. Our aim was to get around Mace Point at that island's eastern extremity, and to drop anchor for the night in the embracing curve of its long, north-facing beach. That challenging eastern point lay only about four miles away.

As the sun dropped toward the mountains of Vancouver Island, however, our following wind had suddenly been replaced by a brisk nor'wester. Now we were closehauled, punching into a head-sea that was rapidly becoming quite steep. The wind strengthened and the opposing chop quickly heightened. We struggled to drive our boats to windward.

Could we thrash our way over the remaining four miles of open water to reach Savary? Perhaps. But *Galadriel*'s bluff bows make rather heavy weather of opposing seas that have become nearly vertical; her progress had slowed almost to a halt. Looking across at Mary on her parallel course a few hundred yards distant, I was alarmed at the duskiness that had fallen between us. The sun had dropped behind the mountains. It would be dark before we could reach Savary at this rate.

All at once the wide expanse of darkening sea around us seemed an empty waste with no readily attainable shelter for the night.

The late-evening gloom settling across the water caused me, for some reason, to muse about the nature of this summer's quest. Somewhere beyond the low, dim barrier of Savary Island lay the beginning of the "northern" waters we had set out to find. And somewhere among the fjords and islands of that coast we might discover what we were looking for: an emptier, quieter place than our more usual cruising ground further south. We both felt that something good awaited us, up among the labyrinthine channels north of Desolation Sound.

Tonight, as *Galadriel* staggered forward against a heavy

curtain of spray, I was a bit daunted by the effort that still lay ahead if we were to reach those remote goals. Even Savary, a scant four miles distant now, hung suspended in the unreachable obscurity of thickening dusk.

I was startled out of my musing by the crash of a heavy bow wave approaching close astern. Mary had steered alongside for a conference.

"We can't reach Savary, can we?" she called above the loud tumble of breaking crests. "But we don't want to spend the night out here. I guess we'll have to give up and run back to Texada."

The thought of losing hard-won ground appalled me. I studied the chart that lay spread on my cockpit floor beneath my booted feet. On the chart, Savary's east point was so very close — only inches away! But even inches are an infinity when you are bouncing up and down in one place, prevented by an opposing wall of seas from making any headway.

"Follow me!" I shouted, taking sudden inspiration from a detail on the chart.

I threw the helm up, eased the sheets, and headed off eastward on a fast reach. *Aiaia* kept pace, her skipper peering across at me with a mild frown of puzzlement.

"Harwood Island!" I yelled.

About five miles inshore from our position out in the Strait of Georgia, Harwood Island nestled beside the British Columbia mainland. Although its distance was greater than that of our original goal, its off-wind direction made it a far quicker, easier destination. With the wind and the seas on our beam instead of on the nose we would fly toward whatever shelter it might have to offer.

The chart detail that I had noticed was promising: Harwood Island culminated in a northern sandspit that curved around a patch of shallow water. At least in tonight's westerly wind, that spit would provide us the anchorage we needed. In the morning, when the season's prevailing southeaster returned, we would have to vacate the place.

With our strong beam wind we covered the five miles very fast. When we tumbled around the spit and rounded up into the shallow bight that lay behind, full darkness had still not quite overtaken us. We groped our way into what we hoped was an adequately sheltered spot under Harwood Island's dark forest eaves. After we had set our hooks into the gravel bottom, we settled for one of our minimalist suppers: baked beans with crackers.

We were exhausted, but too wary to sleep immediately. Although our position close upon the sheltering beach was windless and peaceful, we knew from past experience that wind directions can suddenly change.

It was an interesting place in which we found ourselves. Close at hand on the mainland shore, the Native village of Sliammon was a snug cluster of small houses fading into invisibility in the gathering darkness. The island itself is Native land; we would not venture ashore uninvited. We were grateful for the hospitable shelter of the island's dunes and tall woods.

For the moment we were safe. In the morning, however, the southeasterly wind would almost certainly return, making our position uncomfortable at the very least. Did Mary sleep at all during our night in that place? I know that I did not.

———

The following morning's breeze carried us to Savary Island. In contrast to our previous evening's hopeless slog, the passage to Savary was now swift and effortless. How important it is for the wind to blow in the right direction!

Once we anchored on the shallow sands of Savary's sweeping, tropical-island crescent of beach, we decided to stop for a day of rest. We hoped especially that the night would be a peaceful one, allowing us to catch up on lost sleep. As it turned out, weather conditions that night were supremely peaceful, yet we were not destined to regain much of our lost sleep.

The island's shape — a slender nail-paring fringed with sand — gave it the aspect of one segment of a coral atoll. To Captain George Vancouver's crew, when they first anchored at Savary in July 1792, the place seemed a paradise compared with nearby coastal anchorages that they had found dreary and depressing. When we rowed ashore and walked a circuit of the island on its gloriously sunny sands, we had no difficulty in imagining the restful ease Vancouver discovered there.

This southsea idyll was a feature of real-estate advertising that appeared during the first major development of the island. I remember my father in the 1950s being captivated by this sales literature; for many years Savary Island hovered in his consciousness as a kind of fantasy haven for possible escape or retirement. Someday, perhaps, he would take a serious look at a piece of land on the enchanted isle.

When Mary and I walked the island's roads in the mid-1990s, I was glad that the bubble of my father's daydream had never been pricked by an actual visit to Savary. Only a few paces inland from the serene sweep of the beaches reality reveals itself: an island subdivided into city-sized lots, with their cheek-by-jowl cottages and houses. Along some stretches of the roadway we might have been walking along the suburban street that my father had dreamed of escaping.

Yet it is a quiet place, and a perfect anchorage on a hot summer's day.

After we had walked the tree-shaded lanes for most of a day, we rowed out to our boats. Under the sun-canopy that sheltered *Aiaia*'s cockpit we cooled off with a bucket-shower, washing away the hot road dust with cold seawater. During a leisurely early supper of salad, crackers and cheese we luxuriated in the warm, placid surroundings and imagined ourselves in Tahiti.

Then came the day's first snag. Stepping into my dinghy for another row ashore, I found that one of my oars was gone. I had stowed it carelessly; it had slipped overboard and floated away.

For an hour I rowed Mary's dinghy over a large radius of the anchorage and walked the shoreline in diminishing hope of spotting my errant oar afloat or aground. Finally I gave up. But Mary did not; for another hour she rowed a zigzag pattern over the water, pushing the boundaries of the search outward. I have noticed that Mary's brand of patience (or stubbornness) almost always pays off. In this case, just as evening was settling on the anchorage, her characteristic "yahoo" of victory echoed across the bay.

When she returned with the missing oar, I was delighted. Later, during the hours of darkness, I would find myself even more grateful not to be without that oar.

As sunset approached we went below, aboard our separate vessels, for the night. The stillness was so profound and the sea so motionless that we might safely have rafted together, yet the openness of Savary Island's northern roadstead made us slightly cautious about that arrangement. *Aiaia* lay about seventy yards inshore of *Galadriel* on a surface so transparent and unrippled that it seemed we were suspended in space.

Tonight we would sleep.

———

Then just as the sun slipped from view, another vessel approached. A moderate-sized example of what we sometimes uncharitably call "gin palaces," this high, bay-windowed motor cruiser moved slowly and carefully enough into the bay. After a bit of preliminary circling of the wide, empty anchorage, the skipper selected a spot at which he decided to drop his hook — a couple of boatlengths away from *Aiaia*. I watched critically as he lowered his anchor, snubbing and making fast when his cable had little more than a one-to-one scope — straight up and down. Ah, well, it was a night totally without wind.

I watched until full darkness fell upon us, leaving Mary's boat and that of her overly close neighbor almost invisible. The stillness was profound; nobody was moving. For a long while the couple aboard the motor cruiser sat in dusky profile on their bridge-deck, their quiet conversation accompanied by the uncorking of bottles and the clink of glasses. At last they too retired below.

The previous night's wakefulness was now making itself felt. When I lay on my bunk, sleep came like a hammerblow to the head, quick and deep.

A piercing yell startled me wide awake. It was Mary's voice!

I leapt on deck and strained to see her boat in the darkness. I heard the momentary throb of a powerful marine engine. Mary yelled again — an angry admonition — and the engine stopped. As my sleepy eyes adjusted, I began to distinguish shapes: Mary's little Cal-20 and the towering motor vessel seemingly joined together.

Thankful for my reunited pair of oars I rowed the dinghy quickly across to *Aiaia*, finding on my arrival that, in spite of the nearly total absence of any breeze, the motorized colossus had dragged her carelessly set anchor. That intimidating bulk was almost in contact with Mary's boat, apparently lying afoul of her anchor cable.

"I warned him not to start his engine," Mary cried, adding a bit of language that I will omit here, for clarity. "But he did start it, and now he's got his prop fouled in my

line. In a moment he'll drag both of us ashore!"

The motor vessel's owner, clad only in underwear, stood on his craft's stern-ledge, peering indecisively into the blackness.

"Why'd you need to have so much line out?" he asked, his querulous voice betraying an unsteady slur. Then he dived into the dark water. His wife in her frilly pink negligee hung solicitously over the rail above the transom, belatedly urging him not to risk going into the water. His kicking, thrashing effort beneath the surface resulted, after a few tries, in a loop of Mary's anchor cable coming free of the cruiser's propeller. The loop then settled tightly around an angle of the motorboat's rudder.

Alongside instantly in my dinghy, I worked the turn of the anchor line clear of the rudder on which it had fouled. Then, drawing myself along the cable, I hoisted Mary's anchor into the dinghy. Quickly — as fast as I could row — I carried the anchor and its line away in a great arc, sweeping it clear of the motor cruiser's stern. When the menacing hulk had slid past *Aiaia*'s transom and drifted clear, I rowed Mary's anchor back to a suitable position and dropped it.

We listened to the rumble of the powerful diesel as it retreated slowly into the night. With combined puzzlement and relief we noted that the big powerboat did not stop to re-anchor but chugged its way out of the anchorage altogether.

"Well," Mary sighed, as we sat in *Aiaia*'s cockpit, waiting for our adrenaline rush to subside, "I'm glad I recovered your oar!"

No longer feeling any desire to sleep, we shared a pot of coffee in Mary's cabin. An hour after the incident we were still sitting up in the soft glow of the kerosene bulkhead-lamp. In another hour or so the predawn twilight had begun to dilute the blackness with its first delicate hint of grey.

# Through a Gateway

Once again we were underway, each of us spreading a maximum acreage of canvas to catch the mere illusion of a breeze.

As Savary's beaches fell gradually astern, the gap of Manson Passage very slowly opened to the west of us. Through that window between long spits of sand, seeming very distant in the haze, a most intriguing low islet lay on the Strait of Georgia's reflective surface. A compass bearing identified it as Mitlenatch, a hauntingly lovely little ecological reserve that I had always dreamed of visiting. I gazed at it with yearning. It was far from our intended course for today; but perhaps, someday ...

Like many such plans, my yen for a Mitlenatch visit was destined, one day, to yield a scary experience for us.

Today our plan was to push northward. Ahead lay Hernando Island, and beyond it our day's goal, Cortes.

While our boats idled along on top of their inverted images in the calm sea, I looked across the few hundred yards that separated Mary from me. More strongly than ever in my many years of sailing I felt a sudden wish: how good it would be to cruise in a single boat, and to be sailing together!

While *Galadriel* drifted under an increasingly fiery morning sun, I reflected: this summer's cruise was bringing about a personal evolution. For twenty years my addiction to solo sailing had been almost a pathology. Six months ago, when Mary and I had first cruised in company, both of us were still confirmed loners. Now, however, our shared adventures had begun to dissolve our two solitudes. For a few miles I daydreamed the plans for a new boat, another shoal-draft cruiser like my little *Galadriel* — only not so little!

Gliding in slow motion over the shallows on Hernando Island's east shore, I had leisure to recall a snippet of history about this island. Its first European visitor was the Spanish explorer Francisco de Eliza, in the summer of 1791. Eliza seems to have called the island Campo Alange, but Galiano eventually named it and its larger neighbor to the north after Spanish conquistador Hernando Cortes. Galiano and Valdes sailed these waters in 1792.

As Mary and I engaged in our yard-by-yard struggle to move northward in the day's stillness, I enjoyed a speculation that was to become frequent. I had visions of the Spanish in their engineless, forty-seven-foot schooners *Sutil* and *Mexicana*, crisscrossing these straits and poking into every channel and inlet up this long, convoluted coast. What skillful seamen they were to cover so much ground, in such

waters, with fitful winds, aboard small ships without auxiliary power.

As for us, we were not of such stern mettle. When the wind died altogether, we ran our outboards for a few miles.

A blazing noon found us rafted together at the northeast corner of Hernando Island. While we shared a light lunch (mostly fruit juice, to slake our desert thirst), we gazed over toward the entrance of Desolation Sound. That great branching inlet, selected by many yachtsmen as the ultimate goal and turning point of their summer cruises, has popularly held a special mystique. Only a few miles distant, it offered an attainable afternoon goal for us.

Watching that famous entrance, however, we were not inspired to change course in that direction. Around the Sound's entry-headland at Sarah Point, a steady stream of marine traffic poured. The concentration of vessels — chiefly large motor cruisers — swarming into the inlet was a striking demonstration of many boaters' strange urge to flock together rather than to seek out quiet solitudes. As we gaped at that marine parade from our safe distance of several miles, Mary and I agreed that, at this season, Desolation Sound held no attraction for us.

One feature of the traffic gave us hope. The fact that at least half of the swarming craft were heading southward from Sarah Point seemed to confirm our belief that beyond Desolation Sound we would find an emptier cruising realm. Clearly here we were at the point where many people reach their summer goal and turn homeward.

In the afternoon we ghosted through Baker Passage, around Cortes Island's Sutil Point, and up that island's western shore.

Late in the day we found ourselves in the approaches to the most dramatic of all the harbors we had seen. Before us towered the high, vertical gateposts of The Gorge, the narrow corridor between sheer cliffs that provides an entrance to the two-mile-wide inner basin of Gorge Harbour. Like country bumpkins staring up at city skyscrapers, we lay back to survey the great rock faces that dwarfed our craft as we sailed between them.

Inside, we rafted together to consult our charts. A marina and a government wharf close by the entrance did not look promising; that corner of the bay appeared busy and rather crowded. Our charts showed several side-inlets and shallow coves in other parts of the big harbor. We selected the smallest of them, a narrow notch among rocks not far to the east of the gap through which we had sailed.

When we eased our way between the guardian rocks at its mouth, we found the little cove a perfect place, deserted except for us and a small floathouse that lay on the mudflat back in the inner shallows of the place. I set my anchor in a modest depth of water under sheltering woods. Mary rafted alongside.

In very contented silence we enjoyed a supper of pasta, tomatoes, and Parmesan washed down with a sleepy blend of soothing herbal tea. Soon, cocooned in warm quiet darkness, we slept.

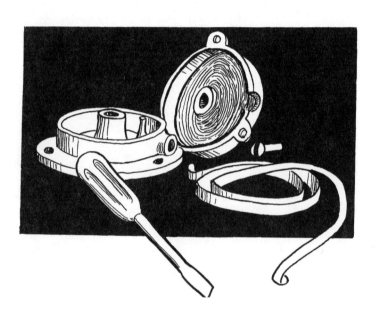

## Dreams and Revelations

The engine repair that I undertook in the morning should have been a quick, straightforward job. But in the first moments of simple disassembly I botched it. My task was a small adjustment to the outboard motor's recoil starter. When I lifted the two halves of its casing apart, I was careless; with a *sproing* like the snapping of a big, low-octave piano string, the starter's coil spring leapt out of its housing and bounced across the deck. I caught it a split second before it disappeared over the rail into the waters of the cove.

After rewinding the spring's very considerable tension back into its housing, I attempted to pull its free end into place on the locking-post inside the casing lid. Like a wild animal, it sprang free. Several more attempts revealed to me a frustrating fact: I would need at least three hands (and preferably five) to restrain the spring and simultaneously reassemble its casing.

For an hour or more I tried a dozen variants of my assembly routine. I concluded each try with a volley of curses as the tightly wound coil threw itself and other parts of the mechanism in a variety of directions.

"That's it, then!" I grumbled. "It looks like, for the rest of this trip, I'm going to be sailing without an engine."

Mary gave me a calm, wise smile. "Maybe you should give it a rest for a few minutes and have another try later."

Before I had begun my mechanical chore, the morning had been gloriously peaceful. Out beyond the mouth of our cove the broader waters of Gorge Harbour sparkled under the touch of a gentle breeze. Into our narrow backwater not a breath penetrated; all was ethereally still.

We had decided this was a good place to lie over for a day or two in order to attend to some practicalities. Across the harbor we would find fuel for our outboards and our cookstoves. Also, with the fresh water from our Lasqueti rainstorm now running low, we would have to replenish our drinking supply here at Cortes.

As an inducement to rest, Mary brewed us mugs of coffee. I was instantly grateful to her for bringing me back to my normal slow pace. Sitting in the stillness under shade trees on the bank close alongside was very heaven this morning.

While we sipped our coffee, we looked at the floathouse, aground on the mud up at the head of our little cove. What an idyllic existence it suggested in its simplicity and relative isolation. At one moment I noticed a face in one of its windows. I gave a small, tentative wave and then looked politely away. When I glanced back, the face was no longer visible. I wondered if the presence of our two small boats anchored in the cove was a violation of the float-hermit's privacy.

We did not go ashore and, throughout our stay in the cove, we remained very quiet.

Quiet, that is, except during my momentary outbursts of frustration with the recoil-spring. During many further attempts to fit the mechanism together, I felt that there had to be a simple, clever way to do it; but the simple, clever trick continued to elude me. On a couple of my tries I came within a hair's breadth of success, bringing the assembly together with trembling hands, only to have the devilish coil snap free of its restraints just before the casing clicked shut. There had to be a secret, and I was too dumb to figure it out. It began to seem certain that, like Galiano and Valdes, I would be exploring these waters without auxiliary power.

———

After lunch we rowed across the harbor to the marina. The half-mile crossing was a long haul in seven-foot dinghies, and it would be an even longer haul back when the little tenders were carrying a load of gasoline and water.

The fuel dock and grocery store were friendly and helpful places, but busy. The jostling crush of boats and people came as a shock; we had forgotten what civilization was like. When we had filled our gasoline containers and our water bottles, we walked in search of Cortes Island's quieter corners. An hour's stroll along somnolent, tree-shaded lanes brought us to Whaletown, a sleepy hamlet whose rustic church, old-fashioned general store, and miniature post office charmed us. We made a mental note of Whaletown's snug harbor, which became a favorite anchorage for us on a later visit to Cortes.

A few hours passed before we returned to the dock at Gorge Harbour. There, a challenge faced us. While we had been wandering the roads and relaxing in the woods, a brisk afternoon wind had risen. Whistling across the broad expanse of Gorge Harbour at about twenty knots from the southeast, it had raised a very dynamic, whitecapped chop. Securely buckling our lifejackets, we climbed into our heavily laden dinghies for the row back to our cove. Soon our oars were bending and our backs straining as we battled to windward, punching against a wet wall of spray.

We pulled with every ounce of energy we could muster. At times the wind allowed us to creep imperceptibly forward over the waves; at other moments we were held fully stopped in spite of our most strenuous effort at the oars. The half mile across to our anchored boats felt like an oar-powered ocean crossing. The sinews in my shoulders burned with the strain, but I could not rest. Our tiny dinghies, low in the water under their loads of fuel and supplies, made infuriatingly slow progress as they inched their way into the wind. I shouted a word of encouragement to Mary, who was bouncing through the slop close alongside.

She asked: "Can we do it?"

We did do it, although we had strained at our oars for an hour and a half to cross the meagre half mile. Safely aboard our boats in the calm of our sheltered anchorage we slumped on deck, exhausted. Eventually, when I had stopped shaking, I lay on my bunk and fell into a deep sleep.

As I slept, I dreamed. In the dream I was holding the several parts of my recoil starter, and I was coiling the spring into its housing. I was doing each step of the process backwards; in my dream I had reversed the series of movements that I had been repeating again and again in my waking attempts to assemble the infuriating little mechanism. The dream-assembly worked easily and perfectly.

Suddenly I sat up in my bunk, wide awake. I knew, beyond any doubt, that the routine I had observed in my dream was the correct one — the secret that had eluded me all morning. Snatching the bag of starter parts from a shelf beside my bunk, I aligned the coil and other bits and pieces in the order in which the dream had indicated. With a satisfying *click* the whole assembly fell together on my first try. A pull on the starter cord showed that the mechanism now worked.

The lesson in all this seems to be that my intelligence when I am awake is about half that of my sleeping I.Q.!

────

In the evening we sat on deck with our supper, watching the bay settle into a glowing, pre-sunset calm. The day's events, however, were not quite over.

We had selected our tiny cove for the attractive fact of its smallness. Narrow, shallow and rock-enclosed, it was a nook that could just comfortably shelter two very little boats. Now, in the quiet of the evening, two very large yachts passed the mouth of our cranny. Seeing us there, their crews decided that the place must be an anchorage.

Into the cove they swept, circling round us in search of enough room to drop their hooks. As they jostled each other (and us), they grew frustrated; they began to yell and curse.

For the first time, we had a glimpse of the float-house owner. He emerged in his lumberjack shirtsleeves and straw hat to glare angrily at the disturbance in his cove. While the shouting, rattling chaos that developed aboard the big yachts engulfed the evening's silence, the resident of the mudflat shook his head in disgust.

Eventually one of the big vessels — the largest — gave up and motored swiftly out of the cove. The skipper of the other boat, moving to a position a little outside the entrance, where the water was deep enough to permit him to swing safely on his anchor line, stopped there. He and his crew settled in to an evening of loud conversation and electronically amplified music.

The floathouse owner watched with his face set in a thunderous scowl.

We woke early the following morning, anxious now to be on our way. When we came on deck we discovered that we were alone in the anchorage. The yacht with the noisy crew had slipped away during the hours of darkness.

After a quick breakfast we hoisted our mainsails and began to haul in our anchor cables. In the very gentle breeze of the early morning our departure routine was easy and unhurried. Mary had her big Danforth anchor aboard first; she drifted around me in a slow arc while I raised my hook and got *Galadriel* moving. We had not started our engines; the breeze provided the quarter knot of speed we needed to get under way.

"Happy sailing!" called a voice from the floathouse.

We both looked in that direction, surprised. The straw-hatted, shirtsleeved man said, "You two, I'm sorry to see leaving. I hope you've enjoyed the cove and that you'll come back sometime."

———

We were on our way, north to Bute Inlet. But before our final departure through the lofty gateway of The Gorge, I was fated to experience a slight embarrassment.

With the wind stiffening now from the southerly quarter, we would need our outboards for the exit, dead to windward in the narrow corridor between the cliffs. Mary had her engine running after one pull at the cord. I was not so lucky. I tugged at the cord of my newly repaired starter again and again. I tried with the choke both off and on. I checked that the air-vent was properly open. After many dozens of unsuccessful tries I changed the spark plug.

My normally trusty Honda would not start.

At last I threw myself on my cruising companion's

mercy. "Mary! Do you think you might be able to tow *Galadriel* out through the gap?"

Mary glanced doubtfully at her own very small outboard motor. But she took the line I threw to her and made it fast to a heavy towing-cleat on her stern-deck.

"I don't know," she shouted. "There's a pretty strong headwind in the gap."

*Aiaia* chugged off, however, very slowly with *Galadriel* in tow. A bit subdued, I sat at my helm watching Mary pilot us out through the eddying tidal stream between the cliffs. In spite of dauntingly stiff resistance from a southerly wind that had now risen to about twenty knots, we crept forward. I watched guiltily as Mary fought the helm, struggling to keep *Aiaia* on course in the swirling current while maintaining a steady tension on the straining towline astern.

I knew we were both thinking the same thing. What if the line broke, or if Mary's engine failed under the added load, in the middle of this turbulent and confined space? It was an awful responsibility to have placed on her shoulders. Eventually, however, we made it.

Outside the narrows of The Gorge we were in a position to turn northwest, to fill our sails and let them draw. With a grin and a thumbs-up signal Mary cast off the towline. A moment later we were raising our big headsails; the two boats turned their quarters to the favoring wind and began the day's run north. Soon we were running fast around the western bulge of Cortes and into Sutil Channel.

It was during our fast, easy ramble northward in Sutil

Channel that I had another of my strange mechanical revelations. I knew why my trusty Honda engine had failed to start. This sudden insight was not something I would be especially eager to share with Mary. On our departure, while I was trying in vain to make the engine start, I might have been more successful *if I had turned on the fuel valve!*

# Sleeping Village

 The place, when we finally arrived there, surprised and delighted us with its strangeness. Like a village under an enchantment — a west coast "Brigadoon" — it lay asleep in the warm reddish light of sunset.

Our boats bumped to a stop against the gentle sponginess of an old wooden dock. When we had cast our lines around pilings, our day's long struggle was at an end. We sat back, slack-jawed with fatigue, gazing in disbelief at the very special landfall to which the close of day had brought us.

The village's cluster of bright little houses nestled on a wooded slope on the very doorstep of Bute Inlet. An architecturally classic, red-steepled, white-clapboard church presided over the silence of the place. We sat unmoving in that unearthly quiet, half expecting to hear the crunch of a footstep on a gravel path or to see a face at one of the windows. But nothing greeted us except the silence of a lunar landscape.

Church House, until not very long ago a busy Native village, had now been left abandoned. At first glance the term "ghost town" seemed appropriate. Yet the place was too neat, too prettily laid out, and too lovingly built to fit the usual image of a ghost town.

During an encounter later that same evening we were to be granted a vision eerily close to my initial "Brigadoon" impression: Church House as a village left to sleep awhile, but soon destined to awake again.

———

Getting here had not been easy.

The first ten miles were gentle enough, except for the abuse I continued to heap upon myself over my outboard motor fiasco. As we ran smartly up Sutil Channel in a handy following breeze, I hung back from *Aiaia*, well out of shouting range, in case Mary should happen to call across to me any embarrassing questions about whether I had solved my engine problem.

By midday we had entered the high-walled corridor of Calm Channel. There at last we were in a world dramatically unlike that of the southern waters in which we had begun our voyage. On either side of the narrow passage, lofty mountains rose to meet a low cumulus ceiling. Ahead, the tall black pyramid of Raza Island was a shape that would seem utterly alien among the gentler contours of the islands further south. The best part of our new seascape was its emptiness. We truly did seem to have left all the marine traffic astern in the region of Desolation Sound to the south.

Before long we began to feel, in the emptiness, an admixture of menace. Our kindly following breeze died, the sky darkened, and from the north a strong wind began to funnel down between the channel's mountainous walls. Soon we were staggering to windward and heaving-to in order to claw down a reef in our mainsails.

As we tacked back and forth against steepening headseas, Calm Channel seemed to have been misnamed. The blackness of the sea and the harshness of the opposing wind gave an impression of our indeed having reached "northern" waters.

As we worked our way past the looming mass of Raza Island, our separate tacks carried us far from each other. While *Galadriel* bounced and crashed through the waves toward the steep wall at the island's edge, *Aiaia* was a thimble-sized toy at the feet of high mountains on the opposite side of the channel. Our boats looked small and lonely in this dark, expansive emptiness.

Finally, toward the end of the afternoon, our opposing tacks brought us together at the north end of a small island in the channel. I sailed alongside Mary to see how she was faring. Typically, she was feeling optimistic. "That little hump a few miles to windward," she shouted. "That's Bartlett Island. If we can get around it, we'll be into Church House."

I gave her an okay signal, and we took off once again, heeling sharply into our separate tacks. As we sailed away, I glanced at my chart. Rather stunningly, the island beside which Mary and I had just rendezvoused was — Rendezvous Island!

A safe haven for the night was now only about two nautical miles away. Like so many of these windward thrashes at day's end, those last two miles felt like a battle to round Cape Horn. Our boats staggered back and forth, gaining precious yards on each tack. A mile seemed a light-year; two felt almost an impossibility.

At last I saw *Aiaia*, a quarter mile ahead, vanish from sight behind the low mound of Bartlett Island. When I rounded the point several minutes later, Mary was on her foredeck lowering her headsail. I was momentarily distracted by the backdrop against which she lay, the colorful storybook setting of Church House, partially hidden amid a green mist of summer shrubbery.

Mercifully, our approach coincided with a sudden drop in the wind. As we glided toward the dock it vanished almost completely.

"The dock is Native property," Mary reminded me. "Perhaps we should anchor rather than tie up alongside."

I thought about that for a moment, but my weariness overruled the usual courtesies. "Let's tie to the dock. We won't trespass further than that."

———

So here we were in the enchanted dusk, still sitting quietly in *Aiaia*'s cockpit after a leisurely supper and a long, slow pot of tea. The place felt very good; we were happy taking our rest under the peaceful old chapel's guardian eye.

Eventually we did venture to set foot ashore, but only onto the dock itself. We walked along the dock to stretch our legs and to find vantage points for good photographs of the village and of ourselves. We moved slowly; our day's long mileage had not been easily won. Noticing a rather smug, triumphant expression on Mary's face as she stood on the wharf, I snapped her picture.

Then I was struck by an anomaly. "Say, Mary! We tied up here over an hour ago. Why are you still clutching that sailbag?" She swayed a little with fatigue.

"What sailbag?" she yawned, her fingers unconsciously tightening their grip on the burden she didn't know she was holding in her hands.

# Calvin, Bobby and Tyrone

 Shortly before nightfall our solitude at Church House was interrupted. A small sportsfishing boat motored quietly into the bay and tied up just across the wharf from where we lay.

Three Native fellows stepped onto the dock where Mary and I were still snapping each other's portraits. The eldest of the trio, a clear-eyed, intense-faced man probably in his thirties, introduced himself as Calvin. When we told him our names, he introduced his younger companions, Bobby and Tyrone.

In the warm, friendly twilight we talked. The three men lived near Powell River, they told us, but they had all grown up here in Church House. They had dropped by this evening after a day's fishing, as was often their practice when they were up in these waters, to bask in the nostalgia of a place they still loved.

"It was good living here when we were young," Calvin sighed. "We are sad to see it deserted now."

"As for us," I explained, "Mary and I have just stopped alongside your dock to rest for the night. We haven't wanted to trespass ashore without permission."

Calvin grinned. "Go ashore! Have a look at our village. I can see that you're people who feel respect for our place. Oh, and another thing: feel free to pick a few baskets of berries."

———

In the still-bright summer dusk we walked up the path between lush walls of blackberry. The first stop on our pilgrimage was a visit to the magnificent little church. Although at close range its structure revealed signs of neglect, the elegance of its architecture was unspoiled by a bit of cracking and sagging. With its steeple leaning slightly, the old building seemed to be resting comfortably in its surrounding cushion of rampant verdure.

We looked down the steep slope to where our boats lay in repose. On the dock Calvin and his crew were preparing their supper over a portable cookstove. A tenuous thread of melody rose up the hillside as one of them sang quietly.

The path branched and meandered through dense thickets and among attractively painted houses — all empty. As we followed the overgrown road in front of the silent houses, we found ourselves listening for children's voices and for ordinary sounds like the clatter of dishware or the slamming of a door.

Mary stopped, listening in an especially focused manner. "I think I heard a twig snap. I'll bet we're not the only ones who are attracted by all these blackberries."

"Bears?" I wondered, somewhat doubtfully.

In response Mary pointed to the pathway just ahead of our feet. A very fresh-looking hillock of droppings spoke more eloquently than any number of words.

We pushed on, drawn irresistibly by the magnetism of the village. In the deepening twilight a mantle of sadness lay over the forsaken houses and overgrown gardens. We advanced slowly but noisily, not wishing to surprise either ghosts or bears.

In a clearing among the tangled vines that had overgrown the whole place we discovered a wall of hanging blackberries. While I was cursing our lack of a tin or bucket to pick them into, Mary had already begun to pluck handfuls of the huge, ripe berries. She hummed contentedly as she dropped her harvest into the obvious container, her inverted sunhat. I tried to hide my own failure of resourcefulness behind a smokescreen question about why she had been wearing a sunhat in the gathering darkness.

The harvest accumulated slowly because both of us were eating ten blackberries for each one that landed in the hat. Eventually I decided to return to my boat for a plastic bucket. Mary stayed behind in the clearing, determined at least to fill her hat.

When I reached the dock and looked back up the hillside, Mary had already finished her berrypicking. I watched her as she stepped carefully down the pathway, balancing her overflowing cornucopia in both hands. Then my eye was attracted by something else moving. A dark, humpy shape emerged from the tangle on the hillside not far above her. I watched as it loped through the dusk, across the clearing that Mary had just vacated.

Mary was less startled than I expected when I told her what I had seen. "After all," she laughed, "Calvin and his people aren't the only berry lovers who claim ancient rights to these lands."

⟶

In payment for our haul of blackberries, Mary presented Calvin, Bobby and Tyrone with a tin of cookies that she had baked just the night before aboard *Aiaia*. As we all sat together in the darkness, munching cookies and popping berries into our mouths, the three men chatted further about their home village.

"You say that you expect to hear voices up in the houses," Calvin remarked. "It's even more haunting for us. When we walk around in Church House, we hear *specific* voices — friends and loved ones who lived in those houses when we lived here."

"I wish we had never left," Bobby sighed.

On this note Mary and I retired aboard *Aiaia* to sleep. Lying in the forepeak berth, we listened with interest as soft guitar music began to waft through our open hatchway from the dock. The three sang with mellow voices, songs with quietly spiritual themes. We listened with pleasure until the singers turned in aboard their boat across the wharf.

We awoke at dawn, eager to hoist sail for the final few miles that would carry us around the last headland that separated us from our summer's destination, Bute Inlet.

In the wan, flat light of early morning, Church House seemed less substantial than it had in the rich gold of sunset. My "Brigadoon" fantasy seemed almost plausible; the village had fallen into a deeper slumber in its comfortable veil of haze.

Its three guardians, however, were up and busy before us. A rather science-fictionish medley of electronic noises emerged as they prepared their high-tech vessel for a day's tracking and catching of fish. Calvin grinned in our direction and then sauntered across to say good morning.

"We're off, up the inlet," he said. "I guess you'll be following us quite a bit more slowly in those little sailboats of yours."

We asked about anchorages in Bute. He shook his head and warned that we might have to sail a long way up the inlet to find any real shelter.

Finally we shook hands. Before turning away, Calvin was moved suddenly to make a last comment about Church House. "The old village is dormant right now, but it's not going to stay like this much longer. I've got a dream about this place; someday soon it will be alive again."

We watched Calvin, Bobby and Tyrone until their boat shrank to a mere dot and then disappeared behind a distant headland.

# Seascape of Another World

Our goal was within reach.

In surreal slow motion, each of us alone with our own joy, we crept around the lofty wall of Johnstone Bluff, just north of Church House. That massive rock pillar was our gatepost; once past it we were inside Bute Inlet.

As we entered, Bute greeted us with a light and fluky headwind. Our progress into the inlet would not be swift.

Here we were, on the threshold of our summer's destination. Months ago when we had pored over the charts, dreaming of this distant place, we had imagined a very "northern" landscape — stormy, dark, cool. The reality today was a surprise; the sun was hot and the sea a rich, tropical blue. The breeze was a southsea zephyr, velvety-warm but too feeble for good sailing.

Ahead of us the mighty fjord wound inland among the

vertical faces of mountains. Its forty-mile length meandered away up to headwaters that we could not hope to reach, tacking against the ghostly-vague summer breeze that opposed us. Even its lower reaches, however, provided what we had come to experience: an awesome solitude.

The morning passed in a dream; we cared little for quick passage to any particular destination.

During a long afternoon drift we zigged and zagged our careless way deeper up the inlet, marveling at the scale of everything in this exotic landscape. We craned our necks to gaze up at ice-streaked peaks and strained our eyes to follow the windings of the passage far into the depths of the mountain fastness.

To the south, no doubt the coves and passages of Desolation Sound still thronged with holiday boaters. Here, in strange contrast, we had sailed into an empty and silent world. We seemed to have arrived on an uninhabited planet.

As the afternoon advanced we tacked against the whispery-light outflow breeze past the high knob of Stuart Island's Henrietta Point. Six miles ahead the inlet curved into the golden haze that slumbered beyond Fawn Bluff. That headland beckoned as a destination that might be reached before nightfall; but against current and wispy breeze we idled without drawing any closer.

I began to give thought to the question of where, in fact, we could anchor when darkness came. In this bottomless canyon of an inlet, where might our hooks find safe purchase?

Gliding together in the mirrored stillness, we held a

conference over our Bute Inlet charts. It was as we had been warned; the deep inlet offered few shallows. We shook our heads in dismay at soundings of more than a hundred meters at the very feet of the fjord's mountainous sides. Behind a small hook of land almost directly across the inlet from Henrietta Point, the chart showed a dusting of fine dots that seemed to hint at a narrow swatch of shallows. With the sun dropping rapidly into the low west, we pointed our bows in that direction.

On a dying breath of air we inched our way across the inlet, our progress now a mere stirring of the imagination. After an interminable drift we approached the towering mountain wall that overhung our intended goal. As we drew close inshore I saw Mary practising her ancient mariner's art of casting a leadline.

"I've found bottom!" she yelled, only a few boatlengths from the shore. "It's seventy meters!"

Tiny boats like ours don't anchor in seventy meters. We ghosted further along the shore, taking more soundings. Finally, almost in contact with the overhanging branches of trees along the bank, Mary called out, "Fifty meters!" The chart showed that we were on top of a narrow gravel shelf, tucked into the angle between two high folds of rock. We rafted together, setting both of our anchors on their full available scope of line.

To remain in place on our precarious gravel shelf we would need to take a line ashore. When Mary offered to row our line to the beach, I gallantly agreed to let her do it; I still had in mind the bear I had seen at our last anchorage.

As it turned out, my cowardice actually did result in Mary being attacked, although not by bears. When she had thrown our long mooring rope around the trunk of a tree and rowed its free end back to our boats, she climbed aboard clutching a painfully swollen hand.

"Bees!" she muttered. "The tree that I picked as our mooring post seems to be their nest."

———

Later we sat at our ease, finishing the last morsels of an enormous meal. In a celebratory mood over our arrival at our summer's goal, Mary had prepared a feast in her two-foot-square galley: a tinned whole chicken, cranberry sauce, fried spuds with sour cream, steamed baby peas, and chocolate cake for dessert.

Over our tea we began to relax sufficiently to appreciate the stunning panorama which surrounded us. The nook in which we lay for the night was a tiny fold in the sheer face of a mountain wall that rose almost vertically from the sea to an impressive height. My chart showed this rampart as nearly 1400 meters — well over 4000 feet.

I stared at Mary, silhouetted against a backdrop of glaciated peaks floating above a void of deep-space blue. It seemed that she was indeed suspended weightless, for the inlet's vastness was devoid of sound or motion. A realization dawned on me: here we were in the solitude that had been our summer's quest.

We floated in a dream, watching the light of the set-

ting sun dwindle from dazzling gold to cool reddish bronze. As the mountains darkened in the twilight, we sat mesmerized, scarcely exchanging a word during the passage of an hour. I felt literally awestruck; the wild, craggy landscape that enfolded us was a scene from some fantasy.

After a long silence I hugged Mary and asked her how she was feeling.

"I'm so happy!" she whispered. "And do you know what really fills me with joy tonight? It is that you agreed to do a cruise in our two boats. What a joy it is to have sailed my own boat to this exciting place. I feel such satisfaction to have brought *Aiaia* here, handling her solo all the way!"

I hugged her more tightly, understanding completely what she was feeling.

As late evening began to cast its shadows across the inlet, we checked our anchors. I was grateful for the profound stillness of the night, because our shelter here seemed precarious. We were secure enough on our narrow ledge of gravel at the foot of the mountain, but I would hate to be anchored in this place during the infamous outflow gales that characterize Bute Inlet in winter.

When full darkness came, it was the true darkness that can be found only in a wilderness place far from city lights. Overhead the sky filled with the constellations of August, brilliantly displayed. Through Cygnus, above our mastheads, the Milky Way cascaded toward the black wall of the mountain ridge under which we lay. Beneath our keels the water of Bute Inlet slept, deep and still, reflecting the night's friendly stars.

We knew tonight that we had come as far north as our summer's voyage would take us. The inlet's deeper reaches beckoned, but my available leave was near its halfway point. It was time to think of turning southward again. And with that thought came my recurring concern: we had sailed hundreds of miles in winds that had been predominantly southerly and favorable for our run north. Would our return voyage be a long struggle against headwinds, a zigzagging battle of hundreds of windward miles to make our way home?

Once again Mary reminded me to "have faith."

Lulled by that thought, we fell into a deep and refreshing sleep in our Bute Inlet haven.

# Dream Archipelago

Drifting about in the neighborhood of Bute Inlet, we quickly became deeply attracted to this region.

When we broke out our anchors at dawn, we began a day's exploration whose impact on our lives we could not foresee. An early-morning ebb carried us down the inlet. We little realized that the next few miles would bring us among islands to which we would soon be drawn repeatedly to return.

The ebb was a blessing, for there was little wind. Our largest, lightest headsails stirred listlessly. Only an occasional bubble trailing astern showed that *Galadriel* was actually moving through the water. Under a cloudless sky we angled toward the chain of big islands that lay across from Bute Inlet's broad entrance. Sailing conditions this day favored a slow, civilized drift down the eastern shore of this archipelago. Directly opposite the inlet we passed a golden, sunwashed headland, Sonora Island's Bassett Point. It looked pleasingly inviting — and unoccupied! Similarly attractive and empty was Maurelle Island, just southward, and, almost in contact with Maurelle, the lush green slopes of Read Island. A thought crossed my mind: these uncrowded lands might be an interesting place to live.

To pass through these islands and to anchor somewhere within them seemed an attractive plan. But where should we make our entry into the group? Mary and I drew alongside each other to consult our charts. A daunting feature of all the narrow channels in this island-crowded vicinity is the power of their tidal currents. For instance, the inviting gap beside which we lay at that moment was Hole-in-the-Wall, through which tumbles a swirling race that can reach twelve knots.

I remembered something from the logbooks of Galiano and Valdes. Sailing through one of the passages near Sonora Island in the summer of 1792, the *Sutil* was caught in the race at full ebb. To the consternation of her crew, their forty-five-ton ship was spun fully around three times before being fended clear of danger by means of oars thrust against the rocky sides of the channel.

Mary, perhaps thinking of similar stories, shook her head doubtfully as she eyed the entrance to Hole-in-the-Wall. (Her caution, as it happens, was somewhat confirmed during another trip to these waters a year or two later. On that occasion we watched a small but powerful tugboat broach and almost capsize while attempting to punch her way through Hole-in-the-Wall against maximum flood.)

"Here's a much easier option," she suggested, poking her finger at the chart. "Let's go through Whiterock Passage; it looks like we'll arrive there just about at low-water slack."

I agreed that Whiterock Passage looked easy. Threading its way between Maurelle and Read islands, it was narrow and shallow, but its typical current was a sedate two or three knots.

We turned southward. And as we separated to move onward, a proper sailing breeze sprang up from the north. As it filled four sails from astern, I remembered Mary's assurance, often repeated during our fast run northward: if we had faith, the summer's long-prevailing southerly wind would change to a northerly when we needed it. Incredibly, the fresh northwesterly that began as we ran down the shores of Maurelle Island prevailed for the following several weeks — long enough to carry us all the way home.

My spirits soared during the quick run along the eastern side of Maurelle. My liking for these islands increased.

Soon we were in the broad entrance to Whiterock Passage. Like a funnel, it closed rapidly to narrows through which we would cautiously pass at low water. We hoped our pilotage would be accurate enough to keep us off the submerged boulders that lined either side of the winding channel. Slowly, with our engines running for insurance, we inched our way through the low-tide shallows. The unspoiled landscapes that passed closely on either side of us strengthened my fantasy of someday finding a place for

myself among islands such as these. This yearning was to haunt me and eventually to draw us back to the archipelago.

Halfway through, Mary had a moment of panic as both wind and engine failed her. While she struggled to clear weed from her propeller, *Aiaia* drifted perilously toward the rocks. At last a timely puff of breeze allowed her a hair's-breadth escape, but when we emerged from the western end of the passage a few minutes later, her face was uncommonly white.

Now we were running down the western shore of Read Island, with a densely wooded little island-cluster, the Settlers Group, close at hand over our starboard rails. As we hurried down Hoskyn Channel in the sheltered confines between Read and Quadra islands, we had left the wildness of Bute Inlet astern. Suddenly we seemed to be "inside" once again, and a door had closed, leaving behind the great fjordland that had been the object of our summer's quest.

———

Our anchorage that night was a delightful place. Still running southward before a moderate northwesterly, we rounded a high, rocky projection called Sheer Point to glide into the sheltered inner basin of Melibe Anchorage. Beside the most truly vertical rock face I have ever seen rising directly from the sea, we lowered our anchors into reasonably shallow water. For some reason, although the place was quiet and protected, we did not raft together. Some unspoken need prompted us to anchor separately, our boats lying in their two solitudes fifty yards apart.

Steep green slopes surrounded us. Rich golden sunshine filtered through tall fir and cedar trees, glowing through into the deep green water of the cove. We walked along the shore, glad to stretch our legs in such a verdant Eden.

Early in the evening, however, the sun set prematurely behind an opaque wall of black clouds. While we ate supper aboard *Aiaia,* huge, leaden drops of rain began to pelt onto the deck above our heads.

"I'd better row back to *Galadriel* before it really starts to pour," I said.

"Okay," Mary agreed, rather sadly. "I guess so."

Strangely, this was to be the mood of our two days' stay in this lovely place. During the night and throughout the following day a torrential and almost continuous downpour confined us, most of the time, to our separate boats. The weather need not have kept us apart, but we seemed to have drifted into our own two worlds. When Mary tried to break the mood, wanting me to be with her, I kept my distance. I was in the grip of an inexplicable depression.

The day after our arrival was spent in a kind of suspended animation. While the rain bucketed down upon us, we walked for brief intervals on the shore or among the woods, but lay during most of the day in our bunks aboard our separate boats, reading or dozing. I found myself back in the lost and self-negating despondency that had paralyzed me during the previous year.

"Even in the rain this snug cove is so lovely," Mary said as we ate our supper together. "Why are you so grim today?

You're spoiling this perfect place!"

The note of censure in her voice startled me into a realization: on this companionable voyage, which had drawn the two of us so very closely together, this was our first rift. I resolved that I would not let it continue. Fortunately, events of the following morning conspired to aid me in that resolution.

# A Visit to the Edge

When the sun rose over Melibe Anchorage's eastern ridge, we saw that hot, dry weather had returned. We raised sail in preparation for departure.

Suddenly Mary gave a shout of distress. Rowing over to *Aiaia,* I discovered her problem. "My rudder is out of action," she pointed out. "Somehow its lower pintle has gone missing."

When I gripped the blade of the Cal-20's rudder, it waggled erratically, unattached to the boat's stern at its lower hinge-point. As Mary had already noticed, a nut and washer had loosened and dropped off and then, somehow, the bolt itself had worked out of its gudgeon and disappeared.

"Perhaps I can find a replacement aboard *Galadriel* ..." I offered very doubtfully.

Mary dived below into her cabin, from which emerged the clatter of her tool drawer being opened. She was back on deck in half a minute, clutching a six-inch stainless steel bolt of hefty diameter. How typical of her to be equipped with a veritable marine hardware store aboard her boat.

She peered dubiously over the stern, however. "The point of attachment is actually underwater. It's going to be tricky."

I asked her to let me have a try. While Mary stood far forward on the extreme tip of the bow to raise the stern a few inches, I inserted the new bolt and worked with my hands in icy water to hold a washer in place while I threaded two nuts onto the bottom of the assembly. It was a slow, fumbling job because my fingers quickly became paralyzed with cold. Finally came the tricky part — tightening the nuts without dropping Mary's vise-grips into the sea. When my hands began to lose their control, we exchanged positions; I became the bow-ballast while Mary completed the tightening. It was a relief to know that, if the vise-grips slipped into the depths now, it would be their owner who was responsible.

When the job was finished, I hugged Mary. Problem-solving always brought us closer together; my depression of the previous day was now swept away in a wave of satisfaction.

Mary blew me a kiss as our boats sailed out of the cove.

As we ran past the lower half of Read Island, southward bound, I returned to my musings about this island chain. The sunlit shore that we had approached on Sonora stuck in my mind especially. But it was to be more than a year before we returned, seeking to establish our own foothold on that island.

As it turned out, we were to explore a remoter possibility first.

———

Not only was the place a remote kind of choice, but the season was unlikely as well. We made our exploratory visit to the Queen Charlotte Islands in the final weeks of a cold winter. Our plan (characteristic, perhaps, of our approach to such things) was to survey the Queen Charlottes on foot, doing the trip as a backpacking and tenting adventure.

While we waited at Prince Rupert for the ferry that would take us across Hecate Strait, we were given a hint of what our adventure was going to be like. Waking in the morning at our campsite near the ferry terminal, we experienced difficulty in pushing open the flaps of our tent. The reason soon became apparent: our tent lay under a drift of deep snow that had accumulated during the night. As usual, Mary seemed unconcerned.

Although the islands, when we disembarked there, were snowless, a true Queen Charlottes-style winter still held the place in its grip. Our first few days' hiking, on the roads and in the woods of the southern island, Moresby, found us slogging through almost continuous icy rain.

As we had discovered while sailing together, Mary and I seemed to get a perverse sort of boost from problem-solving together. Devising a camp that would keep us and our gear dry under the cascading eaves of the winter rain forest was a challenge. Preparing food in the darkness and the wet took special initiative. Mary actually seemed amused by the intricate technology of getting campstoves to burn in the cold rain; lifesaving hot meals materialized just in time to ward off hypothermia.

During our third frigid night in Moresby Island's big woods I cautiously suggested that we might want to consider going home. "What?" Mary demanded. "Are you crazy? We still have three weeks of our holiday left to enjoy."

Another aspect of this excursion, besides the winter weather, was rather daunting to me. I am a sailor, not a backpacker. The weight of our packs, when we shouldered them each morning for the day's travel, came as a surprise. But I was shamed into silent docility by the sight of my slight, doughty companion cheerfully tramping along under a mountain of gear.

Most memorable — because it defied the laws of nature — was a feature of our camp at Pure Lake on Graham Island, the northernmost of the Queen Charlottes. While we huddled in our tent on the shores of that beautiful, half-frozen lake, the temperature plunged. By nightfall the air was a bracing two or three degrees below freezing. As we clung together, our teeth chattering, a thing occurred that defied the wisdom of the natural history textbooks: we were attacked by mosquitoes! Out of the shoreside bog they came, large, whining pests that circled about our heads inside our tent.

I shudder to imagine what Pure Lake's mosquito population must be like in high summer!

Finally our travels, hiking and hitching rides, brought us to the very northern edge of the Queen Charlotte Islands. Standing on the summit of Tow Hill on a day when the weather had suddenly turned warm and clear, we surveyed a breathtaking view of North Beach awash in sunlight.

At the northernmost extremity of this beach, on Rose Spit, we could glimpse the islands of Alaska lying like subtle wisps of haze on the distant horizon.

Along that clean, quiet, sunny beach we found small lots of property for sale. This is what we had come to find. For a day or two we imagined what it might be like to have a place of our own here at the edge of things, and we seriously talked about how we might finance the purchase of a small patch of land.

Yet something else nagged at the back of our minds. In contrast with this stark, wintry northernness, the archipelago of Read, Maurelle, and Sonora islands seemed tropical and southern. We knew that we wanted to return for a closer look at what those islands might have to offer.

———

As we ran south, leaving Read Island astern in the haze of a sweltering summer day, our Queen Charlottes experiment still lay many months in the future. But today we were in something of the mood that we found on that trip. Although we were sailing in our separate boats, we felt the joy of our companionship. At frequent intervals we drew alongside each other to share snacks and fruit juice or simply to talk.

Mary smiled a lot, unable to stop remarking on the gratifying accuracy of her long-held prediction. Her hunch had been right; we were speeding south with our sails spread before a favoring north wind that had settled in just in time to carry us homeward.

# Mitlenatch

 When we had glimpsed Mitlenatch from a distance earlier in the summer, its low, solitary profile had been a lure to us. Now that profile lay directly ahead, tantalizingly suspended on the reflecting surface of an almost windless sea.

Bill Wolferstan in his *Cruising Guide: Desolation Sound* notes that this island's old Kwakiutl name means "It Looks Close, but Seems Always to Move Away." On the day of our attempt to approach it, the island seemed intent on proving the accuracy of its name. While a light, sporadic wind and confusing currents held us under a spell of immobilization, hours of determined sailing brought elusive Mitlenatch no closer. At times I doubted that the island was really there at all; its wispy outline on the horizon seemed merely an ever-retreating mirage.

As we idled along I tidied my boat, folding a scatter of clothing away into waterproof bags and stowing charts that would not be used again during this trip. I shifted my main anchor to a more secure footing on *Galadriel*'s deck, lashing it down so that it could not move.

Handling that anchor triggered a memory of an alarming moment that I had experienced while we were still at Read Island. During the long, depressing day of rain and enforced inactivity in Melibe Anchorage I had noticed that the shallows in which I was lying were littered with a tangle of sunken logs. I decided to move *Galadriel* into slightly deeper water.

When I tried to raise my anchor, I found that it could not be dislodged from a snag on which it had become fouled. After much ineffectual tugging and snubbing at the cable, I attempted an alternative method. I set a small secondary anchor to hold *Galadriel* in place and then used my dinghy to row the main anchor's cable away in the opposite direction. For half an hour or more I pulled at the anchor from a full compass-rose of directions.

Eventually I went over to *Aiaia*. "My trusty old CQR anchor is doomed!" I told Mary. "It's irretrievably snagged. All I can do now is cut its line and at least recover as much of that as I can."

Somewhat to my annoyance, Mary seemed rather amused by my despair.

"I don't think you understand," I said. "It's my main anchor that I've lost — the twenty-pound CQR. Once it's gone I'll never be able to buy another like it; nowadays those plough-style anchors cost hundreds of dollars!"

Mary simply grinned. "Why don't you have another try at it? Sooner or later you'll get it to break out."

"Not a chance!" I groaned. "I've sweated over it for an hour. I've pulled at it from every angle. It's hopelessly snagged."

Nevertheless, on my return to *Galadriel* I gave the anchor line one final, half-hearted tug. A moment later I was back aboard *Aiaia* to report sheepishly that I had retrieved my anchor. It had popped free with scarcely an ounce of resistance. "I wasn't really worried," I told Mary. "I knew I'd get it eventually."

As Mary shook her head and tried to suppress a chuckle, I realized that she was mentally filing away another insight regarding her companion's mercurial personality.

———

A long day passed while we held our course for Mitlenatch. When hunger pangs struck, both of us munched on Mary's latest culinary effort, tasty little snacks based on our friend Doretta's "Welsh Cakes." Cooked up in a frying pan on top of the single-burner galley stove, these bite-sized rollups filled with butter and currants and brown sugar were a handy treat while we clung to our tillers hour after hour.

The hours passed and, finally, Mitlenatch Island's insubstantial ghostliness was replaced by solidity. Perhaps the island truly did have existence in the real world.

During the late afternoon we drifted into the long, curving bight of Northwest Bay. When our anchors were down we surveyed surroundings that seemed like a southsea desert isle. Above the inviting threshold of a sandy beach, the low island itself baked in hot sunshine. The pleasing contours of the place displayed themselves in low-mounded barrens and swatches of scrub woodland.

At first glance we knew that Mitlenatch was worth our long struggle to reach it.

As for the anchorage itself, we realized that it was not really safe. Its placidity on this warm windless evening was deceptive, especially to sailors too weary to drift any further. A slightly better shelter, the tight little nook of Camp Bay across the central flats, on the island's eastern side, already "bristled" with two masts — the limit of that small cranny's capacity.

In the warm glow of evening we walked the paths across the island's fragrant brown-grass meadows. Respectful of this special reserve's delicate ecology, we stayed faithfully to the path, which brought us eventually to an observers' blind above Harlequin Bay. Mitlenatch is the region's principal nesting site for glaucous-winged gulls. We were too late in the season for newly hatched chicks, but from the cover of the blind we enjoyed a view that delighted Mary, a confirmed amateur birdwatcher. Almost at our feet, gull-mothers tended their offspring, fluffily downed young grey gulls that had hatched not many weeks earlier. I had never seen juvenile glaucous gulls so newly past infancy.

For a long while we relaxed, enjoying the peace of simply sitting with the broods of young birds. As dusk approached we explored further, passing the resident naturalists' hut at the head of Camp Bay. It was fortunate that we had not wasted effort in attempting to enter that little haven; the two yachts that lay in its narrow shelter had effectively barred entry to the place with mooring lines taken ashore in a variety of directions.

Back aboard our own boats we were content. The broad northern exposure of our bay posed no imminent threat in the unstirring air of this tranquil summer night.

When darkness fell, a celestial treat lay in store for us. As if to celebrate our arrival at last on the elusive island of Mitlenatch, the annual Perseid meteor shower presented a moderately spectacular display overhead. In its best years this orbiting cluster of space debris pours hundreds of glowing fragments per hour into the mid-August night sky. During our night here in the island's Northwest Bay, at least a few luminous bolides flashed above our top-rigging, providing a good show as we reclined on deck.

It was late when we finally slept.

———

The wee hours found us on deck again. Both of us had been awakened by a sinister change in the motion of our boats. No longer lying placidly on an unruffled smoothness, our craft now rose and dropped precipitously on steep swells that had begun to roll into the bay. We emerged on deck to find a stiff northwesterly wind blowing across the long fetch of open water northward of our anchorage, driving waves of increasing height into the bay.

"We can't stay here!" I shouted.

Mary was already hoisting her mainsail, which glowed grey in the first pale glimmer of predawn light.

Our departure would be a scary maneuver. Pushed shoreward by wind and sea, our boats would be driven quickly back into the surf as soon as their anchors broke free of the ground. We would have to motorsail efficiently to make headway and to avoid being swept ashore. Good seamanship suggested we might be safer to hang on and not risk getting under way at all. But we opted for an attempt at escape while the swells were still a manageable size. Later, if we stayed, they would be large enough to drag our anchors, and then we would be powerless to prevent ourselves from being carried ashore.

After raising my mainsail and starting my little Honda outboard, I hung back, waiting to see *Aiaia* safely under way before breaking out *Galadriel*'s hook. If Mary swung out of control and was swept aground in the surf, perhaps I could let my boat fall back on her securely anchored cable far enough to render assistance.

Mary strained at the anchor until, at last, I heard the rattle of chain and the heavy clank of the anchor itself tumbling onto her foredeck. I sweated in an agony of dread as I watched her dash aft to her tiller, where she quickly sheeted in her mainsail and simultaneously revved her engine. For a seeming eternity the Cal-20 hung on the faces of the inrushing swells, making no headway.

Then I saw her move, just perceptibly, forward. I ground

my teeth with stress; inch by inch Mary drove her boat seaward, putting *Aiaia* through a precarious tack without losing ground. And then, with her sail drawing again after coming about, she began to sail, crawling out past the headland into open water beyond the bay.

As I lifted my own anchor, I hoped I would not suffer the ignominy of wrecking my boat on the rocks after witnessing Mary's skillfully handled escape. It turned out well for me; with my pulse racing I broke free of the surf, which was growing in height with each passing minute.

Many hours later, when we had found a safe anchorage far down the Strait of Georgia, I asked Mary something that I had wondered about all day. "Were you very badly frightened?"

"Frightened? I was so terrified that I almost ... But, you know, somehow my terror seemed irrelevant. While I was trying to get *Aiaia* out of the surf, I was too busy to pay any attention to fear."

# A Payment of Tribute

During all the days' run down the long corridor of the Strait of Georgia we were granted a blessing. Having enjoyed a strong following wind for most of our voyage north, we now reveled in the gift of continuous northerlies while we made our way south. We did some very fast sailing, for it was a vigorous boost that we were being given from astern.

Eventually, in exchange for this swift passage, the gods of wind and sea demanded payment of a small tribute.

For a good part of one week we experienced a veritable catalogue of strenuous days and uneasy nights. At the end of one long run, darkness brought us to a stop in Texada Island's open, westward-facing Mouat Bay. There during a sleepless night we pitched and bounced on the swells from giant cruise ships that churned up and down the strait in seemingly bumper-to-bumper procession.

On another day we were buffeted by a wild maelstrom of high wind and confused seas while we made our way through the narrow passage between Lasqueti and Jedediah islands.

A milestone on our return voyage was the transit of the Strait of Georgia, back to the Vancouver Island side from the sector of the strait nearer to the British Columbia mainland. Sailing westward from Lasqueti's southernmost point we experienced a rough crossing in steep beam-seas whose breaking crests drenched us repeatedly for a period of several hours. Some miles short of our Vancouver Island destination we both yielded to exhaustion; we slipped into the channel between the two Ballenas Islands for a night's rest.

The Ballenas Islands, although not an ideal anchorage, provided an interesting interlude for us. After a cautious approach we dropped our hooks in shallows along the southern island's pleasingly curved north beach. In that position we enjoyed the benefit of at least partial shelter from the nearby northern island of the pair.

It was only after we were securely anchored that I noticed a disturbing footnote in Bill Wolferstan's description of this place: he warned of a submarine cable that invariably snagged people's anchors — precisely in the corner of the bay in which *Galadriel* now lay. (When will I learn to read Wolferstan's cruising notes *before* I enter an unfamiliar place instead of after my hook is down?) I was pessimistic about recovering my costly main anchor, yet I was too fatigued really to care.

After a light supper we rowed ashore. As always, I derived a special pleasure from the simple act of handling *Nutshell*, my trusty old dinghy. This tiny rowboat, which had trailed loyally behind *Galadriel* for thousands of miles, claimed almost as much of my affection as the eighteen-footer herself.

The wind had fallen light and the evening was quite hot.

At the time of our visit, north Ballenas still had a manned lighthouse, but the larger southern island was uninhabited and empty. We found it parklike with its meadows and lush groves of trees. We reclined on a grassy slope in the warm sunshine; our day's heavy labor with sails and tiller had left us lethargic. I suspect we dozed for a while, and when we opened our eyes we were content to remain on our backs, gazing up into the lucid profundity of a cloudless blue sky.

Eventually we walked further over the island's undulating fields. Our stroll brought us among little orchards of neglected old fruit trees, a feature of the landscape that bestowed a kind of gentleness on the place. We were grateful for the contrast between the violence of the strait and the repose we found on this comfortable postage-stamp of land.

At sundown we were in our bunks, where we had a rather fitful night's sleep, thanks to a confused swell that kept the anchorage restless throughout the hours of darkness.

Dawn found us preparing to get under way. I tugged at my anchor line nervously, expecting to find it immovably snagged. The anchor came aboard easily, however, and we were soon outside the cove, setting a southward course.

Out in the open, the wind was strong. We began a run down the Strait of Georgia that remains vivid in memory because of its wild, surfing excitement in tumultuous seas. Impatient now to achieve homeward mileage, we spread maximum canvas, each of us flying a big, lightweather headsail in the thirty-knot wind. Grossly overcanvased, we pushed our little boats beyond their theoretical hull-speed during sprints down the steep faces of the pursuing waves. Miles flashed by as we clung to our vibrating tillers.

It was dangerous to run so fast in such seas, but it was irresistible fun. Vaguely I recalled an old adage: never run downwind with an area of sail that you cannot handle if you unexpectedly have to turn to windward.

Within an hour we were well south of the Winchelsea Islands, six miles from our start at Ballenas. I felt that we might achieve a record passage that day. But it was not without effort; it was a battle to hold *Galadriel* on course while the seas tried to broach and roll her. Not far away, Mary struggled with her boat's helm, clearly getting at least as much violent exercise as I was.

I glanced astern frequently, keeping a concerned eye on *Nutshell*, the dinghy. The antics of that little boat were alarming. One moment she teetered on the crest of a distant wave, at the bitter end of her long tether; a moment later she was surfing forward, catching up and overtaking her parent vessel. I watched for signs of the open boat shipping water amid the tumbling chaos through which she

was being towed. She seemed to be staying on top of everything.

Before noon we were passing Nanaimo Harbour, still well out to sea from the Vancouver Island shore. As often happened during these long, fast runs, Mary had drawn at least a mile ahead. She could never pass up an opportunity to press *Aiaia* to her limits when a strong wind drove from astern.

As *Galadriel* skidded across the open stretch of water between Five Finger and Snake islands, the unusual steepness of the seas induced me to cast another anxious glance back toward my dinghy. I looked back in time to see a breaking crest topple heavily into the little boat, half filling her. I realized that it would take just one more dumping wavecrest to swamp her completely.

Before I had time to take any action, that second great avalanche of water occurred, and *Nutshell* went completely under, at the end of her tow line.

With my huge genoa pulling like a workhorse, I could not stop or slow down. Balancing precariously on the foredeck directly above my boat's smoking, tumbling bow wave, I clawed the flogging headsail down. Then I rounded up and stopped. As I hauled on the tow line to bring *Nutshell* alongside, the submerged dinghy rolled upside down underwater. I heaved on the line, but the dinghy was now as heavy in the water as the carcass of an elephant.

Each time the sunken dinghy dropped behind the ridge of a passing wave, the line snapped taut with a jerk that almost carried me over the rail into the sea.

Finally I faced reality. My attempts to recover the little boat in these turbulent waters might actually cost me my own life. I cast off the tow line and left poor *Nutshell* to settle into the waves astern.

Meanwhile Mary had seen my struggles and was beating back against the thirty-knot wind to come to my aid. As she drew near, turning to surf toward me across the wavefronts with the wind abeam, a sudden combination of wavecrest and gust rolled *Aiaia* flat in an almost total ninety-degree knockdown. Even at a distance I could hear a smash of crockery — and a colorfully phrased curse!

A moment later she was upright and sailing again. As she drew alongside she cried, "I've broken my favorite china mug!"

———

In the afternoon we made a safe arrival at our familiar anchorage among the Flat Top Islands.

One of the richest pleasures of small-boat cruising is the blessed instant when the bonejarring motion and the cacophony of noise end, and suddenly you are at peace in a still, silent place. In the glassy shallows behind the barrier of the islands we relaxed and drew breath.

We were glad to be safely at anchor, but I was sad about the loss of my trusty old *Nutshell*. Judging by her gloom I noted that Mary regarded the demise of her favorite mug as an equal catastrophe.

I was philosophical: "We've been given this charmed voyage, with following winds and swift passages. I guess we can't complain if a small tribute has been charged in exchange."

*Home Waters*

One day we slipped through Gabriola Passage to find ourselves back in "home waters" after our long sojourn in wider spaces.

On this occasion we did Gabriola Passage in the recommended manner, waiting until slack water before proceeding through the narrows. This channel's maximum tidal velocity of about eight knots does not match the violence of some of the big rapids further north. Nevertheless, it can be a dangerous place because of the tendency of the race to sheer sideways, carrying small craft into the rocky shallows.

While passing through this region during another sailing trip a year or two later, we gave ourselves a scary ride through Gabriola Passage. Trying to reach the Flat Top Islands at the end of a long run up Trincomali Channel, we arrived at the western entrance to the passage at an hour when the current was still at full flood.

Mary voted to wait. I was impatient to let the flood sweep us right through. "After all, it's only a knot or two faster than the current down in Baynes Channel, and we routinely shoot that race at full flood."

I led the way and Mary followed. The first half of the passage was easy; we enjoyed the high speed that the strong tide and a following wind gave us. In the final narrows, however, we found ourselves engaged in a life-and-death battle for control. Where the rapids curled in a tight curve that collided with a large obstructing rock, we motorsailed desperately to negotiate the dogleg turn and to claw ourselves away from the obstruction that lay directly in our path.

As we broke free of the current's malicious clutches, we met a procession of huge motor cruisers bent on punching their way through the narrows at high speed, against the tidal race. In an instant their turbulent washes had flung our little craft back into the rapids from which we had just escaped.

By the time a repetition of our first struggle had eventually got us safely clear again, we had learned much about the reasons for choosing slack water for a transit of these narrows.

On our return from the Bute Inlet voyage we tackled Gabriola Passage in a manner that was more seamanlike and neatly timed. We idled through at high-water slack, reaching the western mouth of the passage in time to catch the first of an ebb that would carry us down Trincomali Channel.

In contrast to the wild openness of the Strait of Georgia, the narrow waters of Trincomali Channel, among the southern Gulf Islands, seemed cozy and familiar. I felt a surge of affection for this intricate marine landscape that had for many years been a world sufficient for my peaceful driftings under sail.

At day's end, however, we would make a discovery that I had somehow missed in my decades of small explorations: we were to be delighted by a meeting with Old Stoneface.

The wind in Trincomali was very light. We were rather impatient with our slow progress because, for the first time during the summer, we had a deadline to meet. We had decided on an experiment that would prove to be fun. At one of the harbors a day or two previously, Mary had phoned her sister Aggie, who lives in the Northwest Territories. On a whim we had invited Aggie to fly south and to join us in the Gulf Islands. Intrepid (and trusting) soul that she is, she agreed to find her way to the islands and to come aboard at Long Harbour on Salt Spring.

I myself am less trusting where high-precision arrangements like these are concerned. I prayed that wind and tide would bring us to Long Harbour in time to meet Aggie's ferry there. The planned rendezvous was now just three days away.

Mary, of course, felt no concern; she was navigating on her usual faith.

———

The very light breeze eventually carried us into Pirate's Cove on De Courcy Island. Although that popular anchorage was far from deserted, we found quiet elbow-room in the shallows down in the cove's southern mudflats.

In the rich evening light we rowed along the island's sculptured sandstone shores. Having lost *Nutshell*, I was lucky still to have my handy inflatable tender. Pirate's Cove was unruffled; unmoving branches overhung the shore, mirrored in the dark water below. It was while we idled beneath these forest eaves that we meandered into the narrow backwater over which Old Stoneface presided. I was a little startled to glance up into the weathered old face that daydreamed under the shade of a slouch hat at the water's edge.

He raised no objection — in fact, took no notice at all — while I sketched his portrait.

———

The following day's light autumnal breeze carried us all the way down to Annette Inlet on Prevost Island.

During that quiet drift southward, at a speed that only occasionally rose above two knots, I did small housekeeping chores aboard *Galadriel*. I tidied lockers that the past week's wild sailing had reduced to a jumble. I rolled my sleeping bag into its nylon storage-shell. I discovered a pair of shoes that had lain in bilgewater for two months. Why I had brought shoes on the summer's voyage I am not sure.

Since our departure I had worn seaboots or sandals or nothing at all on my feet. Halfway down Trincomali I threw the sodden shoes overboard. Strangely, I have never owned a pair of shoes since. After that long summer of living chiefly barefoot or sandaled, I have never again been able to tolerate the constriction of shoes.

When we anchored at Annette Inlet, I breathed a sigh of relief. The Long Harbour ferry terminal lay across a two-mile-wide passage from where we lay for the night. Our rendezvous looked like an easy prospect now.

Mary's feelings as we relaxed together in the familiar haven of the inlet were mixed. "It will be exciting to have Aggie aboard; I can hardly wait! But the leg of the voyage that she'll be sharing with us is the last. She'll be sailing with us for only a few days before our summer adventure comes to an end."

As it turned out, however, the last few days held a lot of fun in store for us — and a rediscovery of the gentle magic of islands close to home.

*Rendezvous*

When the three of us sat down to our first supper together aboard *Aiaia*, there was an air of improbability about the meal. In the almost semitropical warmth of a southern Gulf Islands anchorage we tucked into an arctic banquet of caribou meat.

To Aggie, whose passion is cross-tundra dogsledding, caribou is pretty routine fare. To Mary and me, her gift of our first evening's supper was an exotic change from beans, pasta, and green salad from island gardens.

I wondered how Mary's sister would adjust to our some-times uncomfortable life aboard the little boats. As the two women reclined in the cockpit, excitedly keeping an eye on an eagle perched on a nearby branch while they washed down their caribou with large mugs of coffee, I realized that they were two of a kind. The thought crossed my mind that, in such company, perhaps I might prove to be the least adventurous of the three.

Our rendezvous with Aggie had itself been a test of her adaptability. Few ferry passengers are normally met in the fashion of our pickup earlier in the day on Salt Spring Island.

Somewhat daunted at first by Long Harbour's apparent lack of anchorages, we sailed slowly up and down the narrow corridor between its high rock walls. Eventually we found a tiny, but perfect, enclosed cranny directly across the inlet from the ferry terminal. I doubt that most yachtsmen would regard this diminutive notch in the wall as an anchorage; we found it snug enough to accommodate our two vessels—just barely.

When Aggie disembarked from the ferry, she probably little suspected what she was getting herself into. In view of our arrangements for meeting her, we were relieved to find that she had arrived with no luggage except one substantial backpack. To her puzzlement and consternation, we led her to the brink of a cliff, then proceeded to scramble down the steep incline to where our dinghies lay suspended on top of large boulders at the water's edge. Aggie showed no surprise when we explained that the next step would be a long row, in these tiny eggshells, across the inlet to the distant shore where *Galadriel* and *Aiaia* could be seen at anchor.

Mary transported the heavy backpack in her dinghy, while I carried her sister in mine. Any doubts about Aggie's ability to be comfortable afloat quickly vanished as we balanced knee to knee in the small inflatable tender whose stability depended entirely on neither of us blinking or sneezing.

Late in the day we sailed back across to Annette Inlet for the night. As we approached the spot at which we planned to stop, Mary pointed out *Aiaia*'s anchor, where it lay ready on her foredeck, and began to explain how it should be handled and set. "I'm pretty familiar with anchors," Aggie said. "Up in the north we use them with the dog teams. Sometimes it can take a well-set anchor and a good scope of line to bring a strong team to a stop."

During two or three days of mild breezes and warm, early autumn sunshine we pottered among islands whose quiet loveliness we experienced freshly through the eyes of our guest, who was cruising among them for the first time. We were grateful that the gentle weather gave Aggie a chance to adapt to life under sail without any scary acrobatics. Yet, as the sisters drifted along aboard *Aiaia*, Aggie began to ask Mary when we were going to have some real wind.

At D'Arcy Island we went ashore on a beach that curved beneath outreaching trees that looked like tropical jungle. Here, for me, was the essence of home waters, an island under whose shelter I had anchored scores of times over the past quarter century. As we hiked around the island's perimeter to gaze southward down Haro Strait, a shock of realization struck me. Here, at the end of our summer's wanderings, we had only about eight miles left to sail. Our home bay could actually be glimpsed beyond a headland that lay indistinct in the mist, away to the south.

For supper on this last night of our voyage both Mary and Aggie insisted on one special delicacy. For them, nothing else would suffice. "Fresh crab!" Aggie demanded. "It was my main reason for coming down here to the BC coast."

While I snoozed on my bunk aboard *Galadriel,* Mary and Aggie lowered their crab trap into the cove. I was skeptical about their simple faith that we would have a crab dinner within an hour.

An hour later we sat aboard *Aiaia*, forking huge pieces of freshly steamed crab from a pot that bubbled invitingly on Mary's stove. Dipped in hot lemon-butter and eaten with fried bannock, the just-caught crab was undeniably the finest delicacy of our entire voyage. When the sun lay red on the western horizon and then disappeared in a crimson haze, we rocked gently beside D'Arcy's darkening beach. This warm, still, twilight hour was as perfect as any that we had enjoyed during the long summer.

The following morning brought the stiff headwind that Aggie had begged us to find for her. I beat my way southward in close company with *Aiaia*, whose crew grinned and laughed with the pleasure of these few challenging miles of Haro Strait. I noticed that Aggie was not intimidated by our wet progress through steepening head-seas; in fact, at times she confidently handled *Aiaia*'s tiller while Mary relaxed beside her.

What joy I felt, watching the sisters sailing Mary's well-travelled little ship homeward.

I half-awoke in the middle of the night and, glancing out, caught a glimpse of branches silhouetted against the dark sky. I leapt from my bunk in alarm. I thought: "Oh, no! *Galadriel* has dragged her anchor; she's right inshore among the trees!"

Then I woke fully and remembered. It was not in my bunk aboard *Galadriel* that I had been sleeping. I was in bed, in a house. We were afloat no longer.

*Epilogue*

On one of those everlasting evenings near the summer solstice, Mary and I walked up a steeply sloping, grassy roadway bordered by silvery alders. It was late, but the alders' billion leaves shimmered in a warm, lucid glow.

At the crest of the road we turned aside into woods. We were now threading our way among great trees on a path of our own making, overhung by branches that rang with birdsong even at this hour. We stepped across a small stream on a crude log bridge that we had laid over the trickle of clear water. Not far beyond lay the colorful wedge of our small tent, dwarfed by the giant hemlock at whose feet it nestled.

My lifelong dream of islands has been strange in one respect; always I have sailed among islands like a ghost, tantalized by the beauty of the islands, loving them, but having no place among them that I might call my own. To be adrift under sail, always on the move with no specific destination, has been a delight that was perhaps most appropriate to my youth.

With the passage of many years I have felt a subtle change: the growing yearning for a patch of ground somewhere among the islands on which I could step ashore and rest in a place that I could call my own.

When we went north up the straits again and returned to the islands that lie in the approaches to Bute Inlet, we had come on a venture that might prompt some to think me naively foolish. We were on Sonora Island to enjoy our first look at a property that I had already purchased — sight unseen.

As we sipped a late-evening tea, side by side on a log in front of our tent, I thanked God for His kindness to naive fools. Our little acreage was a parkland that rose up through fine woods to a level-topped rock mesa behind our campsite. Earlier in the day, on the brow of that flat ridge, we had identified the perfect site for a small cabin.

———

Later in the summer we found ourselves spending dream-days on Sonora Island. During many sunny afternoons we stood on the ridge, mentally constructing a cedar deck on its south-facing clearing and designing the simple A-frame cabin that would someday be built on the deck.

We idled away hours every day simply lying in the grass

on the nearby shore, mesmerized by the tranquil vista of thronging islands in a calm summer sea. It was a place where we seemed unconscious of time, whose passage on those hot windless days was languorous and unreal. Sometimes we sat on the dock, in desultory conversation with islanders whose cabins lay hidden among the trees up behind the bay. Nobody seemed in a hurry to go anywhere; a somnolent mood prevailed.

The shores of the bay were green, warm, quiet. It was a good place. For a long time I had yearned to have my own small share of a good place.

What had I been searching for during all my explorations among the byways and backwaters of these broad straits? Henry James once asked Robert Louis Stevenson the motive behind his explorations. A paraphrase of Stevenson's reply serves very well as my answer also: "I want someplace that suits my need. For me, there must be boats, and there must be islands!"

...n Hydrographic Service
...ment of Fisheries and Oceans